Night [...]
bene[...]
said t[...]
to prove [...] doubters that you're the
best eventing horse in the whole world."

The big bay stopped his nervous dancing
and suddenly became intently interested
in the far line of trees that edged the
meadow around the practice ring.

"I know," Kate said. "I wouldn't mind a
trail ride myself." She bit her lip, thinking
how super it would be to race the tall
horse across the field just for the fun of it.

Night Owl made a rumbling sound deep
in his chest and danced sideways, catching
Kate's excitement.

She turned the horse toward the gate,
leading him to the open woods beyond
the farm. Kate forced Night Owl to keep
to a walk as they passed the barn, and
then finally gave him his head.

Night Owl responded immediately,
stretching himself out in long, free strides,
his powerful muscles rippling under a
mahogany coat that glowed in the afternoon
sun. They thundered across the long
meadow, Night Owl's hooves beating against
the soft grass. The sound filled Kate with a
wild joy as Night Owl streaked toward the
woods, and by the time they reached the
edge of the meadow, Kate was laughing
out loud.

RIDING HIGH

Chris St. Johns

FAWCETT GIRLS ONLY • NEW YORK

RLI: VL: 5 & up
      ───────────
      IL: 6 & up

A Fawcett Girls Only Book
Published by Ballantine Books
Copyright © 1989 by Cloverdale Press, Inc.

Library of Congress Catalog Card Number: 88-92193

ISBN 0-449-13450-4

Manufactured in the United States of America

First Edition: April 1989

Chapter 1

SIXTEEN-YEAR-OLD Kate Wiley concentrated on circling her horse around the ring. She moved easily in the saddle, in rhythm with Night Owl's trot, which at the moment was faster than it ought to be. Frowning, Kate pulled in the reins.

"You're moving too fast," she told the tall bay thoroughbred. "We're schooling for dressage, not the Kentucky Derby." She swiped at a wisp of long, blond hair that had pulled loose from her single braid. "All right," she went on. "Let's try it again, and this time try not to act like your tail is on fire." Patiently, she set him trotting alongside the rail again.

Kate and Night Owl were eventers, which meant that every time they competed in a show, they had to prove themselves in three separate events—stadium jumping, running the difficult cross-country course, and performing exacting movements in the dressage arena.

Eventing demanded endurance, courage, and all the skill a horse and rider had. And for Kate it demanded something more—a level of perfection that she'd never quite reached. There was something way down deep inside her that made her want to be the best. When she took Night Owl to a show she expected to win a ribbon, and if she didn't, she couldn't help feeling as if she'd failed.

Kate's dream was to one day ride in the Olympics. She knew it would take years to make that dream come true, and she was willing to work hard for it. But she was only half the team. Night Owl had to be willing, too, and so far today he was anything but.

"Pay attention," she said sharply as the horse's pace picked up again. She closed her fingers tightly around the reins and sat deep in the saddle, both cues for Night Owl to slow down.

Night Owl shook his big head. "You want me to go slower?" he seemed to ask. "How's this?" and he dropped his pace to a walk.

"That's not what I asked for and you know it," Kate said, reining him to a stop. "We're supposed to be trotting, Night Owl, one–two, one–two." She counted out the rhythm for him.

"Better," she said, and continued to call out the rhythm. "That's better." They made one complete circle before she could feel him picking up speed again. She reined him in and sat for a minute drumming her long fingers on her knee. Her blue eyes turned toward the house. She hoped her mother would come out and tell her what she was doing wrong, but there had been no sign of her mother all afternoon.

Kate, a slim blond girl with delicate features, sat chewing her lower lip. "You know," she said to her horse, "a lot of people don't think you can do this dressage thing. They say the novice level is as high as you can go." Night Owl nibbled the bit, listening.

"Well, we finished all the novice tests last season, Big Bird, and you did very well. You did better than very well. That last event, you were super."

She paused a minute, savoring the memory. No one had been surprised when the Owl came in with the fastest time on the outside course. And no one had been surprised when he completed the stadium jumping class with no faults. Night Owl's strength was his athletic ability. But when he scored a seventy in the dressage tests ... well, half the spectators fainted.

Night Owl bobbed his head up and down as if he were remembering, too. "You were surprised, too, huh?" Kate said. "To be honest with you, sweetie pie, so was I." She patted his withers. "I was stunned. But that just goes to prove we can do it if we put our minds to it." This year, they were moving up a whole level, competing at training-level, the first level of intermediate competition. It meant they had to work harder and faster and better.

Night Owl snorted and moved restlessly. "Okay, then," Kate said. "This year we're going to prove to all those doubters that you're the best horse in the whole world."

The big bay stopped his nervous dancing and suddenly became intently interested in the far line of trees that edged the meadow around the ring. The trees marked the start of the trails that crisscrossed the woods beyond the Wiley farm. The treetops were shaded a delicate green against the bright blue April sky.

"I know," Kate sighed. "I wouldn't mind a trail ride myself, but it's too late today." Night Owl made a grumbling sound deep in his chest. "Course, we could take a *short* run." She bit her lip, thinking how super it would be to race the tall horse across the field just for the fun of it.

It was spring, and the long, cold Connecticut winter was finally gone. Overnight, the slushy pile of snow on the north side of the barn had disappeared. And so had the cold fingers of wind that had found the small of her back no matter how many sweaters and down vests she piled on.

Kate was itching with early spring fever, and Night Owl probably was, too. That might even be why he was being so hard to manage. "I'll bet you've got a whole winter's worth of stored-up energy underneath that shiny coat," she said. "If I let you run today, will you be good for me tomorrow?"

Night Owl rumbled again and danced sideways, catching Kate's excitement.

"Besides," Kate rationalized, "Mom will be able to work with us tomorrow. Coach Mom always knows how to fix things."

She turned Night Owl toward the gate. He moved forward impatiently, but she held him in check as they crossed the drive and skirted the front lawn. Her mother had this thing about hoof prints in the flower beds. Kate forced him to keep to a walk as they passed the barn, and then finally gave him his head.

Night Owl responded immediately, stretching himself out in long, free strides, his powerful muscles rippling under a mahogany coat that glowed in the afternoon sun. They thundered across the long meadow, Night Owl's hooves beating against the soft grass. The sound filled Kate with a wild joy as Night Owl streaked toward the woods.

This wild ride was not the sort of thing you could do with most horses, but Night Owl was special. He had been Kate's for four years, and in that time they had formed a relationship like no other Kate had ever shared with a horse before, and she'd known a lot of them. Kate couldn't remember a time when she hadn't ridden. Her parents had always had the stable, and Kate had grown up around horses. But never a horse like Night Owl. There was a connection between them she couldn't explain, a kind of magic.

Kate settled back and pulled lightly on the reins, barely a touch. Night Owl responded and came down through his gaits, from the gallop to the trot and finally to a walk. At the end of the meadow he came to a complete stop. He wasn't even breathing hard. Good, Kate thought. That meant that after the long winter he was still in shape—even if his powers of concentration in the ring weren't what they should be yet.

Night Owl stretched his neck out and shook his head. "Now what?" he seemed to be asking.

"Impatient, are you?" she asked, grinning. "Okay, let's see what you're made of." She turned him back toward the stable and the long line of low hedges that separated the big meadow into small fields. His whole demeanor changed; she could feel him tense. "You like this idea, don't you?" Kate said. "Me, too. Let's do it!" She leaned forward, half out of the saddle, and hugged his withers. As the hedges came up, she judged the distance, steadying the horse, pacing him. He gathered himself under her and sailed over the hedge with a foot to spare, then took the next and the next and the next. By the time they cleared the last one, Kate was laughing out loud. She brought him from a canter to a trot, then headed him toward the barn.

"That is how it should be," a voice called to her from the parking area, "freedom and fun!"

Kate turned in the saddle to see the small, rugged figure of Pietro Yon watching her. His hands were deep in the pockets of the old, brown jacket he always wore. Pietro was an old family friend. He'd once been her mother's coach when her mother was showing, before she had her accident.

"He has wings," Kate called to him happily.

Pietro laughed and nodded his head. Wiry gray hair framed his face, weathered and creased from a life spent outside. "You are almost as good as your mother was."

Kate knew that was high praise. Pietro always said Anne Wiley was the best rider he'd ever coached—and he'd coached some of the best. Pietro had been a riding instructor in Poland before the war and had once done some work in Austria with the Lippizaners. Then he brought himself and his talents to America, to Smithfield, Connecticut.

"Are you staying for dinner?" Kate asked.

Pietro nodded. "I could never say no to one of your mother's dinners."

"That explains why my mother was too busy to work with me today. She's probably been inside cooking up a storm."

"And who deserves that kind of attention more than me?" he asked innocently.

"I'll see you inside." Kate laughed and turned Night Owl toward the barn.

Her chores done and Night Owl back in his stall, Kate ran quickly up the worn stone path to the old farmhouse. In the small entryway between the back door and the kitchen, she pulled off her work boots and set them on the floor next to her mother's. She tried not to look at the empty spot where Popsie's bed had been. Kate missed the big sable collie. Her mother promised that someday soon, now that spring was here, they'd be getting another dog. Not to take Popsie's place, of course. It just was nice to have a dog on the farm.

Kate shrugged out of her ragged barn-coat and padded barefoot into the kitchen, where her mother was putting the finishing touches on a salad. Kate fished a carrot stick out of the bowl.

"Wash your hands first," Anne Wiley scolded, tapping the back of her daughter's hand.

"I'm starving," Kate complained. "When's dinner?"

"As soon as you've had your shower." Anne added cucumber slices to the salad. "Pietro is here."

"I know," Kate said. "I saw him outside. Is Dad home?"

"Yes, the two of them are in the den watching the news and waiting for you, so scat." Her mother moved from the counter and stopped at the window to look outside. "Somebody's just pulled in the drive," she said.

"It's probably Mr. Jesper," Kate said, sneaking one more carrot stick and smiling impudently when her mother turned and caught her, "checking on Time-Out." Time-Out was one of the Wileys' boarders who was due to bear a foal some time this spring.

Mrs. Wiley stood for a minute watching, one hand on her hip, as the car moved slowly toward the barn. She was almost as tall as Kate, and just as slim. Her hair was a darker gold than her daughter's and cut much shorter. It was obvious that they were mother and daughter, the resemblance was so strong. She turned and said to Kate, "Jessie didn't come today?"

Jessie Robeson was Kate's best friend. She didn't have her own horse, and for the last two years she'd leased Time-Out. But now that the mare was about to become a mother, the Jespers had told Jessie she wouldn't be able to ride her anymore.

"No," Kate said. "She doesn't come as often since she can't ride. I feel so awful for her, Mom."

"I know," her mother said and sighed. "Jessie's had some rough times."

Rough times, for sure, Kate thought. Jessie's mom had died less than a year ago.

"If only she had her own horse," Kate said. "It'd help a lot, I just know it would."

Anne smiled sympathetically. "Jessie's dad has enough on his mind right now without having to worry about that. A house and three children to take care of without any help? That's a heavy load."

"Jessie does a lot," Kate said, defending her friend.

"I know she does, honey." Anne sighed. "And I wish we could help her."

"Do you have an idea?" Kate asked hopefully.

"Nothing that's a real solution," Mrs. Wiley said and kissed Kate on the cheek. "I love you for caring so much. How did Night Owl behave?"

"Not very well."

Her mother stopped what she was doing and gave Kate her full attention. "What's wrong?"

Kate shrugged. "We're probably just suffering from starting a new season. Why don't you come out to the ring tomorrow and watch us go? You can probably put your finger on what's wrong in a minute."

"I meant to come out today," her mother said apologetically, "but there's so much to do to get ready for spring, and then Pietro called. . . ."

"That's all right," Kate said. "We can do it tomorrow."

"If he wasn't going well, why didn't you work him longer in the ring? I saw you out in the fields and thought you were rewarding him for a good schooling session."

"No, it wasn't a reward," Kate said. "He wasn't listening, and I was getting upset, and I thought a good run would cool him out so he'll be better tomorrow."

"Kate," her mother said emphatically, "if Night Owl has a weak spot it's his ring work. That's what you have to concentrate on. His running and jumping doesn't need any help at all."

"I know." Kate twisted the end of her braid between her fingers. "But I never can seem to get things going in the ring by myself. I need you or Jessie. We'll work like slaves tomorrow, I promise."

"You'd better," her mother warned. "The first show is only a few weeks off. Now go take your shower. All this food is making me hungry."

Kate padded into the hall and was halfway up

the stairs when she heard her father's voice. "We're hanging on by our fingernails," he was saying. She stopped, listening. "That indoor ring we're adding is going to use up what little profit we make and then some," he said.

"But you need an indoor ring." Mr. Yon's voice was heavily accented with conviction. "It's good for the farm. And Kate cannot make it to the top unless she can school year round."

"I know," her dad said, "and that's why we're putting it up. Only now we've got to find a way to pay for it."

"Keep your nails hanging just a little longer," Mr. Yon said. "Kate is moving up a level this year, no? Now is when the scouts, the team captains, the professionals come looking to see who's coming up."

Kate heard her mother enter the hallway from the kitchen. "Aren't you in the shower yet?" she asked in exasperation.

"I'm going. Don't run the hot water," Kate said, and scampered up the stairs. She grabbed some clean clothes from her room, then went into the bathroom, stripped, and waited for the water to run warm.

Scouts, team leaders, pros—Mr. Yon's words rang in her ears. She might be discovered, like a movie star.

"*You*, young lady"—she made her voice deep and masculine sounding, and it echoed in the tile bathroom. Pointing at herself in the mirror, she said, "We have our eyes on you. Keep up the good work. You're headed for the Olympics."

Still caught up in the fantasy, she grabbed a towel and draped it over herself. But it was no longer a lavender bath towel—it was the same American flag that the hockey goalie had draped around himself when the United States team had beaten the Russians at the Winter Olympics.

Goose bumps rose on her skin and tears pricked her eyes—right there in her own bathroom with the shower running. Imagine how she'd feel if it really happened. "They'd probably have to carry me up to the winner's stand on a stretcher," she said, then giggling to herself, she stepped into the shower.

The warm water felt good on her back and neck, but her worries returned. Her mom was upset because she hadn't kept Night Owl working on dressage in the ring today. Kate soaped up a sponge and scrubbed her legs, trying not to think about how poorly Night Owl had responded to her today. She wished the first show wasn't so close.

Then the awful thoughts started. What if last year was the best they would ever do? What if the people who said Night Owl couldn't make it at the higher levels were right? Or maybe she wasn't good enough to bring out the best in him.

Lately, Kate had had nightmares about the spring shows. In the worst ones, she and Night Owl entered the dressage arena, and she couldn't remember the simplest thing.

"You're being a dork," she said aloud as the water cascaded over her face. "Mom says I'm good; Mr. Yon says I'm good. They can't *both* be wrong. And *I* know that Night Owl's the greatest."

Besides, she had a secret weapon: her mom, who was the greatest coach around, as far as Kate was concerned. She was right there whenever Kate needed her. So what if training was a little rocky at the moment? Her mother would help her smooth it out.

Chapter 2

"I'LL have some more meat." Kate held her plate out across the dinner table.

Marc Wiley, Kate's father, groaned. "Where does she put it?"

"Riding's hard work," Kate answered.

"Never for you," Pietro said. "For some people yes, but for you it is like breathing. And just as important. Am I right? Don't answer, I am right. I have an eye for that kind of talent. Your mother had it." He looked at Mrs. Wiley and raised one thick eyebrow.

Kate knew what was coming and waited, grinning a little.

"She broke my heart, your mother," Pietro said.

"I also broke my leg and my collarbone," Anne Wiley said, and laughed. "He conveniently forgets that part of it."

Pietro dismissed her words with a wave of his hand. "You could have ridden again. Bones heal."

Kate knew there was nothing her mother could say to that because it was true. Bones did heal. But something besides bones had been broken inside Anne the day she'd had her accident.

"Maybe I have another chance," Pietro said, looking at Kate. "She's almost as good as you were."

"She's better," Anne said.

"In some ways," Pietro agreed, studying Kate.

"She's got the determination," Marc Wiley said, "and the spirit."

Pietro was still watching Kate. "She gets what she wants with elegance. Some riders, you know, they pull, they push, they use brute force. Kate isn't like that."

"Could we please stop talking about me as if I weren't here?" Kate asked, blushing.

"You don't like to hear how good you are?"

"No," she said honestly. "It makes me feel weird."

"Why?" Pietro asked, surprised. "I used to beg people to tell me how good I was."

"Forgive me, but you *were* a ham, Pietro," Anne said, "and Kate, God bless her, is a nice unspoiled young lady, which is how we'd like to keep her."

"She will be better than you." Pietro said, "I make a prophecy." He tapped his forehead. "She knows more than she knows she knows. People like that make the best riders, because when they need that little bit extra—*pop*, it comes right into their heads."

Kate laughed. She loved the way Mr. Yon talked.

He smiled at her. "I was waiting for you to make a place for yourself on the North American Young Riders Championship Team. Then I was going to step in and take all the credit."

"You would do that, too, wouldn't you?" Anne said, and grinned.

"I would," he agreed. "Except"—he paused and looked around the table—"I am retiring."

Kate, Anne, and Marc all stared at him, their jaws open. "Never," Anne said.

"Always and never," Pietro said with a sad smile, "are two words that should always never be used."

"But why?" Anne's voice was soft with surprise. "Why retire now?"

"My health, my age. I can't get the help I need and I refuse to accept less than perfection when it comes to caring for the horses. You know that."

"I do," Anne said.

"But you'll miss it," Kate said. Pietro Yon's whole life had been horses and riding.

"I will miss it," he said simply. "But there's no way around it."

"But you're well, you're fit—you're the healthiest person I know," Marc protested.

"My doctors tell me I won't be if I keep up this pace. For myself I don't care. But my wife—it isn't fair to her not to listen to my doctors. So, my dear, dear friends, we *are* going to close the farm, sell the horses, and retire to Florida."

Kate looked at Pietro's face and saw the sadness there, and the signs of tiredness and age she hadn't noticed before. She glanced at her mother and knew that she'd seen them, too.

"Florida!" Anne Wiley said. "So far away! We'll miss you."

Pietro grinned. "Then you will spend your vacations in Florida."

"*Vacations?*" Anne looked blankly at her husband. "What are *those*?"

"Don't worry," Marc said to Pietro, "when I explain what they are to her, she'll want one."

"I'm counting on it," Pietro said. "I will hold you to that." Then he took a deep breath and held his hands out in front of him. "Now where is that apple pie I smelled baking?"

"Well," Kate said after Pietro had gone, "that was a bombshell."

"Not really," her mother said. "I've seen it coming for a while." She and Kate were in the dining room, clearing the table. "I'm glad he's listening to reason for once in his life. He's probably the most stubborn man I've ever met."

"He really meant that, about you breaking his heart, didn't he?" Kate said.

"I think I'm probably the only student he ever had that said no to him." Anne took a stack of dishes into the kitchen, and Kate followed.

"Mom?" Kate said, piling dishes on the side of the sink, "why *wouldn't* you jump again? I know, it was a bad fall, but what Mr. Yon said is true. The bones healed. And you ride dressage."

Anne ran water into the sink and took a long

time to add just the right amount of detergent. "I felt so responsible for the horse," she said finally. Kate knew that the horse Anne had been riding had also been injured in the fall, but unlike Anne, there was no way his injuries could be cared for. They'd had to put him down. "At least I think that's the reason," Anne said, plunking a pile of dishes down into the suds. "How's the homework situation tonight?" she asked, abruptly changing the subject.

"Awesomely awful," Kate said, and groaned. "I've got a math test tomorrow. And I completely forgot about a book report that's due on Friday. Know any good, short books?"

"Kate," Anne said sternly, "I hope that cutting your school day short isn't getting to be a problem." Kate had an arrangement with her school that riding fulfilled her physical education requirement, and her stablework was part of an independent study. That made it possible for her to leave school an hour earlier than the other kids. Usually she was back at the stables by one-thirty.

"No. The book report is my fault; I just plain forgot about it. I'll go talk to Mrs. Rottman. She's pretty good about extensions."

"Why don't you forget the dishes, then, and get started?"

"Five minutes won't make that much difference," Kate said.

Her mother had even less free time than Kate did. Running a stable the size of Windcroft, with ten horses you were responsible for, was a twenty-four-hour-a-day job. There was always something that didn't get done. When they were finished with the dishes, Kate knew, her mom would go back out to the barn to make sure the horses had all been fed and watered and had clean bedding for the night, and that none of them had taken sick between the last time she'd seen them and now. Then she'd go to bed and worry that something would happen to one of them before she had a chance to check them in the morning.

"Okay," her mother said, letting the water swirl down the drain, "that's it for tonight. You go do your homework." She dried her hands and headed for the back door. "Did you by any chance check the schedule to see who needs the blacksmith? He's coming on Friday."

"Yup," Kate said, setting a stack of dishes up on a shelf. "It's the regular group and Miss Molly. She threw a shoe yesterday. I didn't know whether to turn her out or not, so I left her in."

"She can go out," Anne said. "She just shouldn't be ridden until all her feet are balanced. Poor baby, she won't like being cooped up."

"Poor baby, my eye," Kate retorted. "She's a royal pain—the Houdini of horses when it comes to getting out of closed places."

Anne laughed. "That she is. Maybe the chain and padlock Dad put on the gate will hold her in." She opened the kitchen door and slipped her feet into her boots. "Just keep telling yourself, Miss

Molly pays a lot for the privilege of staying here. It makes almost anything bearable."

Kate heard the back door close and in a minute heard it open again. Her mother poked her head back into the kitchen. "Katie May," she said, using her special nickname for Kate, "come out here."

Kate slipped the last of the cups and saucers into place and walked out on the back porch with her mother. "Listen," Anne said.

Kate's face broadened into a happy smile. The night was filled with a high, piping sound. "Peepers," she said, listening to the call of the small frogs that heralded the coming of spring to Smithfield, Connecticut.

"I guess it's officially spring," her mom said, wrapping an arm around Kate's slender waist.

Kate looked at her mother's fine profile, and saw sadness in her eyes. "You're going to miss Mr. Yon, aren't you?"

Her mother nodded. "He's like part of the family. But we can't be selfish and try to hold him back. I'm sure the decision to move was probably the hardest one he's ever made. The nicest thing we can do for him is not make it harder." She hugged Kate and headed toward the barn.

The moon was coming up, and near it the evening star shone brightly. Kate looked at it and whispered her childhood plea, "Star light, star bright . . ." She wished for many things. She wished that her dream might come true, that she would turn out to be as good as Mr. Yon and her mother thought she was, and that, with her help, the farm would be successful and her parents could stop worrying.

They were big wishes, maybe too big for even a star to handle. Besides, it would take more than wishing; she knew that. It would take work, a lot more hard work before the spring competitions. She finished the little rhyme and took one last breath of the fragrant night.

Chapter 3

KATE held the refrigerator door open with her knee and pulled out the orange juice, butter, and eggs. One of her regular duties was making breakfast. Her long hair was brushed loose and flowed down her back in long, shimmering waves.

"Morning, Katie May," her father said as he came into the kitchen. He was wearing his blue suit and striped tie.

"My, look at you," Kate said. Marc Wiley ran his own computer consulting firm from an office in the house, and most of the time he dressed in slacks and sweaters. A suit and tie definitely meant something important.

"I'm meeting with a new client today. Keep your fingers crossed."

"Okay," Kate said, doing as she was told. She ran the water in the sink and listened while the

ancient pipes groaned and wheezed and then de-
livered a thin stream of hot water. Her mom and
dad sometimes got upset with the old house's
odd ways, but they didn't bother Kate a bit. She
didn't mind at all that the stairs squeaked and the
floorboards were splintery and the doors and windows all hung crooked. She loved every nook and
cranny of her home. It was a friendly place, old
and lovable. She didn't spend any time worrying
about leaking roof shingles or disintegrating stone
foundations, or the money they took to repair,
but she knew her father did.

"That hot water system is going to have to be
replaced," he said, and sighed. "What do you say
we chuck this place and move into a condomin-
ium?"

Kate whirled to look at him, aghast.

"Just kidding," he said.

She turned back to her work and broke two
eggs into the frying pan. "I can't imagine what it'd
be like, living in a condo, or even one of those
plain old houses in town."

Her father laughed. "Probably like a vacation."

Kate stirred the eggs and without turning around,
said, "Like a vacation to Grossville."

"Don't worry, Katie May," her father said, "I
love this old house same as you do, and I love the
animals. I just wish they all didn't cost so darn
much."

"We're not in trouble, are we?" Kate asked,
suddenly remembering the conversation she'd
overheard between her father and Mr. Yon.

"Not to the point where we have to worry," her father said.

They were almost finished with breakfast when Anne Wiley came in from the barn.

"You're finished early," Marc said.

"Yes, there wasn't much to do. Some angel" —she looked at Kate—"got most of the morning chores set up last evening."

Kate smiled. "I had some time. That's one of the things Jessie used to do," she said.

"She's such a sweet kid," Anne said, pouring herself a cup of coffee. "And a fine rider.... Katie," she added thoughtfully, "would you tell Jessie that if she wants to come out today, she can ride Jonathan. I'm not going to get the chance. But no jumping."

"Not even *little* jumps?" Kate wheedled.

"Not even *little* jumps, and none for you either. I want to see you in that ring doing dressage exercises."

"Yes ma'am," Kate said, and saluted.

"Well, I'm off," her father said, and kissed Anne on the cheek and Kate on the top of her head.

When he was gone, Kate poured herself another glass of milk and drank it slowly.

Her mother, across the breakfast table with her coffee, watched her closely. "A penny for your thoughts."

"I was just wondering about riding Night Owl at a higher level this year." She raised her blue eyes to her mother's. "Do you really and truly think I'm ready?"

Her mother studied her a long moment. "What *I* think isn't nearly as important as what *you* think."

Her mother was right, of course. Trouble was, Kate wasn't exactly sure what she thought. "It's just that I get this truly gruesome picture sometimes, of all the other kids doing better than me," Kate said.

"All what other kids?"

"You know. The kids I've been showing with since pony club."

"Kate Wiley," her mother started to say sternly, but the telephone rang before she could finish.

She didn't have to finish. Kate knew exactly what her mother was going to say: *You are not in competition with anyone but yourself. Do the best you can and don't worry about anyone else.* Her mother had been telling her that for years. It was easy to say, but hard to do if you liked to win as much as Kate did.

Anne came back grinning and poured herself a bowl of cereal. "Guess what? That was a call from a stable in Pennsylvania, wanting to know if we had room for another horse."

"Pennsylvania?" Kate said, impressed. "How'd they find out about us?"

"They didn't say. The connection was pretty bad. But they said they'd call back to let us know if the horse was coming. I'll find out then. So," she said, "we have to get all the boxes and stuff out of one of the empty stalls. And it looks like I'm going to be too busy to do much riding for

the next week or so. So tell Jessie she'll be doing
me a favor if she takes over that chore for me."

"You're just saying that to be nice to Jessie,"
Kate said, smiling.

"Partly," her mother admitted. "But remember,
no cross-country or jumping today. I want to see
a solid hour of ring work."

"Maybe some little jumps after?" Kate coaxed.

"Just in the ring," Anne said. "Oh!" She reached
behind her and pulled something out of a pile of
mail on the sideboard. "With all the excitement
yesterday I forgot to give you this." She handed
Kate a small red, white, and blue booklet. Across
the top in big letters was written, *USCTA Schedule, Spring Horse Trials.* It was the listing of the
events scheduled for the coming season for the
United States Combined Training Association.

"The schedule!" Kate cried. You could talk about
the season starting all you wanted to, but when
the schedule came, the season suddenly became
very real. "I'll look through it on the bus—which
I'm going to miss if I don't get a move on." She
downed the rest of her milk in a gulp and, grab-
bing her books, raced out the door.

Running down the road to the bus stop, all the
worries she'd had over the last few days were
gone. In their place was pure joy. In her hand she
held a little book that would tell her where she'd
be and what she'd been doing for most of the
weekends this summer. And what she'd be doing
would be what she loved more than anything else
in the world—competing with Night Owl.

In past years Kate and Jessie would pore over the schedule, looking for farms they loved to show at, laughing over memories of shows that had not gone quite as expected.

But this year, she thought with a start, Jessie probably wouldn't even want to see the schedule. Because this year, with Time-Out in foal, Jessie had no horse to show. Oh, if only Jessie's dad would get her a horse of her own!

The school bus pulled up, its red lights flashing, and Kate clambered aboard. She was greeted with hi's and hey's, and waved back to her friends as she settled into her seat. Immediately she opened the schedule.

There were changes in the dressage tests, which she'd have to memorize. The tests would be longer and more difficult than last year's. She'd expected that. But, expecting it and feeling comfortable about it were two different things. Of course, she thought, if Jessie could come out to the farm to ride Jonathan they could work together. There was a lot that they could help each other with. Kate smiled at the thought of her friend, who didn't care how long it took to teach a horse the right way to do things. Those times when Jessie had been able to show, she didn't care if she didn't place, as long as she thought that at each show she had done better than the time before.

It was probably the best way to look at showing, Kate thought with a sigh. It certainly was a more relaxing outlook than the one she was stuck with. But, Kate admitted, grinning to herself, it lacked the excitement that wanting to come home with a blue ribbon every time supplied.

She flipped through the schedule, reading the locations of the trials. There were events scheduled in Connecticut, Vermont, New Hampshire, and New York State, all close enough for them to van the horses.

"What is that thing, a cheat sheet?" Bruce Davidson was peering over her shoulder. Bruce was a short, well-built boy with red hair and a quick, nervous way of talking. "You've had your nose stuck in it since I got on the bus."

"It's the USCTA schedule for the spring shows."

"Oh, that horse stuff," he said. "I was hoping it was the answers to the math test. Did you understand that stuff? I was up half the night studying."

"Most of it," Kate said.

"Then you're probably the only kid in the class that did," Monica Norton said from across the aisle. She ran a small hand through her short, dark, curly hair. Her blue eyes were frowning. "You and Amory."

Kate was drawn into a discussion on the impossibility of geometry. She closed the schedule and slipped it into her notebook. She'd look at it again at lunch, with Jessie. For now, she'd stop thinking about horses and talk about school.

Amory, Monica, and Bruce were part of the group that Kate hung around with in school. There was also Pete Hastings, who had missed the bus today, and Jessie and Kristin Clarke.

Sometimes Kate felt as if she were two separate

people. One Katherine Wiley lived at Windcroft Stables and rode horses, and the other Katherine went to school and worried about grades and felt bad sometimes because she missed out on so many school activities. It wasn't that she didn't try to be more a part of things at school. It was just that riding and schooling the Owl took so much time. And there was so much else to do at the farm. If she had to give up something, there was no question in her mind what it had to be.

The bus wound through the streets of the sleepy little village of Smithfield and turned into the parking lot of Smithfield Regional High School. Bruce and Monica fell into step with her. "So, when's your first show?" Bruce asked.

"The end of this month."

"Do you do that jumping stuff?"

She squinted at him with annoyance. "It's not *stuff*. You make it sound silly."

"Well what *do* you call it?"

"Do you really want to know?" Kate asked, turning to face him. So many times the kids had asked her about what she did, only to lose interest the minute she started to explain it.

"Yeah, I really want to know. Would I ask if I didn't?"

"Sorry," Kate said. "I don't have a lot of patience on the subject of my riding. Nobody in school takes it seriously."

"Who cares if nobody takes it seriously?" Monica teased. "You get to wear those super outfits that make you look like English royalty out for the hunt."

Kate sighed and turned off down the hallway toward her locker.

She caught sight of Jessie and, waving, called to her. "How come you didn't come to the farm yesterday?"

Jessie hooked her shoulder-length brown hair behind her ear. She was almost as tall as Kate, with the same slender but muscular figure. "There really wasn't any reason to. Besides, I had to go to my grandmother's for dinner."

"A *special* dinner?" Kate asked, drawing the words out a little.

Jessie nodded and her aristocratic face broke into a smile. Because of her looks, a lot of people thought she was stuck up, until she smiled and they saw the fun and friendliness in her eyes.

"Roast leg of lamb?" Kate asked again, more slowly.

Jessie nodded, laughing.

"Why don't you tell your grandmother that you hate roast leg of lamb?"

"Because it's the *only* thing she can cook without burning." Jessie's grandmother had been a radio actress and had never quite learned the homey arts.

"I guess she means well," Kate said.

"She does. And, you know, I don't know what I'd have done without her after Mom died." Kate could see that it still hurt Jessie to talk about her mother. She drew a finger along the edge of her notebook. "You know, you never realize how many things you need a mother for. At least I didn't, but

Gram's always there, every time something comes up. Sometimes even before I know I need her."

"You just wish she'd learn to cook something besides leg of lamb."

"Yeah," Jessie said, and grinned.

"Well I've got news that will wipe the memory of last night's dinner right from your mind," Kate said.

"Time-Out had her foal and Mrs. Jesper said I can ride her again," Jessie guessed.

"That wouldn't be *news*, that'd be a *miracle*."

"I know, but I can't get too excited about anything else."

"You will about this," Kate insisted, and, in a rush, told her about Jonathan. "And it'd help me a lot if you came out and rode with me while I'm working with Night Owl."

Jessie was still taking it in, wide-eyed, when the bell rang. She started to move away.

Kate grabbed her arm. "So you'll come out to the farm this afternoon and ride Jonathan?"

"Jonathan," Jessie said. "Really? Look, I've got to get to history."

"Say yes!" Kate cried.

"Absolutely," Jessie managed. Grinning, she rushed down the hall. "We'll talk at lunch okay?"

Kate beamed at her. "See you at lunch," and she sped around the corner, feeling great.

Chapter 4

KATE pushed her tray along the counter in the cafeteria, inspecting the day's offerings. She selected a salad, a dish of spaghetti, and a piece of pie for dessert.

"Why don't you get fat?" Monica, who was on line next to her, muttered. Monica was forever on a diet.

"I don't know," Kate said. "But whatever the reason is, I'm happy about it." Kate had a lean, athlete's body, spare and muscular. Sometimes she joked with Jessie that they had bigger biceps than some of the boys they knew—that's what working with horses did for you. When she was in seventh grade, Pete Hastings had challenged her to an arm wrestling match, and she'd won.

"What are you grinning about?" Monica asked, reaching for a salad.

"I was just thinking about the time I beat Pete at arm wrestling."

"Kate," Monica said with authority, "you *never* beat boys at *anything*. That's the first cardinal rule."

"Cardinal rule for what?" Kate asked, presenting her lunch ticket to be punched by the cashier.

"Getting asked out on a date."

"I don't have time for dating," Kate said, a little too sharply.

"*That* I will never understand," Monica said, rolling her eyes toward the cafeteria ceiling. "What else *is* there in life besides dating?"

At their usual table, Bruce and Pete Hastings were already halfway through lunch. Pete was a tall, blond boy, with sparkling brown eyes and a smile that sometimes made Kate wish she *did* have time for dating. Next to Jessie, Kate thought Pete was one of the nicest people she knew. She sat down and searched the room for Jessie, but didn't see her.

"Where's everybody else?" Monica asked.

"Amory's absent," Bruce said. "I don't know where Kristin and Jessie are."

"Jessie's making up a test," Monica said. "I saw her in third period."

"She is?" Kate said. "Funny, she didn't tell me that. And we've got something important to talk about."

"Let me guess," Bruce said. "Your horse picked the winning lottery number."

Kate made a face at him.

"Not funny," Pete told him.

"I thought it was funny," Monica said, and Bruce grinned at her gratefully.

"If you hurry up we can get a Frisbee game in before lunch period's over," Bruce said.

"I'm done." Monica popped the last cucumber slice on her plate into her mouth.

Everybody's eyes shifted to Kate. She still had a mound of spaghetti to eat. "If you all stare at me," she said, putting down her fork, "it'll take me forever. Why don't you start without me? I want to wait for Jessie anyway."

"Want me to wait with you?" Pete offered.

"Thanks, but that's all right. You go ahead and play."

Monica nudged her hard.

"That hurt," Kate hissed.

"You have *so* much to learn," Monica moaned. Kate guessed that the second cardinal rule was not to say no to a boy if he asked for the chance to spend time with you.

"Come on, you guys, let's go," Bruce said.

Pete shook his head. "It's not going to be much of a game with just the three of us."

"Jessie and I'll come out as soon as we eat," Kate promised.

"Don't forget," Pete said.

"I won't. See you later." And Kate went back to her lunch.

She was finished with the spaghetti and working on dessert when Jessie arrived and sat down next to her.

"Where is everybody?" Jessie asked, rummaging in her lunch bag.

"Playing Frisbee," Kate said. "Eat fast and—"

"Forget Frisbee," Jessie said, and took a bite of her apple. "I want to talk about Jonathan. Did I hear you right this morning?"

Kate went on placidly eating her pie.

"Kate," Jessie warned, holding her hands in an open circle in front of Kate's throat.

"Okay," Kate said, and laughed. "Mom said you could ride Jonathan, since she doesn't have the time. I didn't have to push her at all. She actually said you'd be doing her a favor. She's so busy she hasn't had a chance to ride him at all this week."

"And I can ride this very afternoon?" Jessie asked, happiness flooding through her.

"Yup. Oh, Jessie, it'll be super to have you work out with me. I'm so stressed out, working on my own."

"What're you stressed out about?" Jessie asked, finishing up her sandwich.

"Oh, Night Owl's being a drudge, and I really do need you riding with me, at least while I'm schooling. He seems to have forgotten everything he ever knew about dressage."

"You're not exactly on your own, even if I'm not there," Jessie said in her reasonable way. "Your mom's always there."

"True. But I need you both. Besides, you're my good luck charm."

"Well that's me, all right." Jessie sat back in her chair and beamed at Kate. "I'm the best good luck omen around. But so is your mom. I thought my afternoons of riding were over." She gave Kate's arm a happy squeeze. "Tell your mother I love her."

"She knows," Kate said, picking up her tray and depositing it on the collection counter. "Bring your apple outside, the Frisbee team awaits."

Kate hoisted herself up on the grain bin and dug a chocolate chip cookie out of her pocket. She took a bite and checked her watch. It was almost three. Jessie should be coming any minute. Tramp, the barn cat, jumped up beside her and eyed the remains of the cookie. "What a beggar you are," Kate said, and broke off a small piece for him. She popped the rest of it into her mouth and drained the last mouthful from a can of soda.

"Kate?" Her mother's voice came to her from along the row of box stalls.

"Coming," Kate said, and jumped down from her perch. As she walked, she pulled her long hair forward over one shoulder and deftly braided it.

The barn was a simple structure, one long aisle with box stalls opening on both sides. There were fourteen stalls, though only ten of them were filled, three with horses that belonged to the Wileys. Her father always said that if they could fill all the stalls, even if they had to hire some barn help, the farm would pay its own way. But filling all the stalls wasn't as easy as it sounded.

"What do you think?" Anne said, standing in front of an open box. "Is that swelling gone?"

Kate hunkered down, securing the end of her braid with an elastic band, and then examined the right foreleg of a small, friendly, jet-black mare. The mare lowered her head as if to search Kate's blue eyes for an opinion.

"Oh, yes," Kate said. "It looks a zillion times better."

"That's what I thought." Kate could hear the relief in her mother's voice. "Okay, my pretty," she said to the mare, "you get to go outside and play."

"I'll take her," Kate offered, pinning her braid to the back of her head with a gigantic barrette that her father referred to as "the car door hinge." She clipped a lead to the mare's halter and led her down the aisle toward the door. The horse's hooves made sharp ringing sounds on the cobbled surface. As they passed Night Owl's stall, his ears came forward and he grunted deep in his chest.

"Don't be jealous," Kate told him. "This'll only take a minute, and then the rest of my day is yours." She ran the mare out to a paddock, watching closely to see if she favored her foreleg. She didn't, and satisfied that she was sound, Kate turned her loose. The mare ran halfway into the paddock, stopped, raised her nose to smell the sweet air, shook herself, and dropped her head happily to crop the new grass.

A scrunch of bicycle wheels on the drive told Kate that Jessie had arrived.

Mrs. Wiley came out of the barn, a bridle in one hand.

"Will you have time to watch us ride today?" Kate asked hopefully as they waited for Jessie to reach them.

"I'll try," her mother said, and sighed, "but I can't promise."

Before Kate could say more, Jessie came running up to them. "Mrs. Wiley," she said breathlessly, "thank you so much. This is the most fabulous thing anyone's ever done for me."

"You're quite welcome," Anne Wiley said, smiling. "And you're the one who's helping out. I guess Kate told you—I just don't have time to ride Jonathan right now."

"I'll treat him like he's gold."

"Just treat him like a horse and you'll be doing me a favor," Mrs. Wiley said, and gave Jessie a hug. "There's nothing worse than a riderless horse." She handed Jessie the bridle. "I was going to tack up Jonathan, but now I'll leave that to you, Kate," she said, turning unhappily toward her daughter. "I know I haven't spent much time with you, but ..."

"It's okay," Kate interrupted her. "I know you're busy. But first chance you get?"

"First chance I get," her mother promised, and hurried back into the barn.

Jessie and Kate followed, and when Night Owl heard them he whinnied in greeting. "He knows every time you're coming," Jessie said.

"Yup."

"Time-Out did that for me," Jessie said. "I wonder how long it will take her to forget me?"

"She won't forget you, Jessie."

"Yes she will," Jessie said matter-of-factly. She went over to Time-Out's stall. "Someone else will be taking care of her, and riding her—and showing her—and she'll get to love that person. Won't you, Time-Out?" The mare whickered softly.

Kate couldn't stand it when Jessie talked like that; it was so sad. "Here we are, Big Bird, just like I promised," Kate said, trying to sound cheerful as she clipped a lead line to his bridle and cross tied him in the aisle.

Then she started her daily ritual of grooming, beginning with a currycomb to loosen any dirt in his coat. Night Owl's neck relaxed, his head dropped, his ears pointed at right angles instead of standing up straight, and his eyes closed drowsily. Being brushed was one of the things he loved best in all the world. Kate was almost finished before Jessie left Time-Out's stall and brought Jonathan out to be groomed.

"So," Kate said between strokes of the currycomb, "did Time-Out have anything interesting to say?"

"Just that she misses our rides and that she's getting tired of being an expectant mother. Boy, is she big," Jessie said, working hard to get Jonathan's coat clean. "I wonder whether she'll have a filly or a colt? Hey," she said suddenly, "pretty soon, I'm gonna be a grandmother," and they laughed.

Kate reached for a hoof pick and carefully cleaned the delicate area of Night Owl's feet where stones and bits of debris were apt to collect, then handed the pick to Jessie.

"How is he to ride?" Jessie asked as she worked on Jonathan's feet.

"John-boy? He's real easy," Kate said. "He's got a canter like a rocking chair; you can ride him all day and not get tired. And he listens. Mom's got him really well trained."

Kate gave Night Owl a last swipe with the brush and stepped back to look at him. His mahogany red coat gleamed and his black mane lay neatly to one side. Now that Kate was finished fussing over him, his head was up, his neck arched. She had to tilt her head to look up at him. She whistled and his ears pricked up. She never stopped being thrilled at the sight of him. He was so big, and strong, and wild-looking, even though he was a pussycat at heart.

"He's gorgeous," Jessie said softly.

"Yes, he is," Kate agreed.

As if he knew they were talking about him, Night Owl stretched out his neck and shook his head in agreement. Kate tacked him up, then turned to Jessie. "Ready?" She grabbed her practice helmet.

"Almost." Jessie buckled the last strap of Jonathan's bridle. They led the horses outside and mounted.

"How does he feel?" Kate asked as they walked, then trotted, the horses in the ring.

"All right," Jessie said. "It's kind of early to tell."

They were riding alongside the rail, Night Owl in the lead, Jonathan following like a lighter, more golden shadow.

"We'll do a diagonal," Kate called over her shoulder, "and then try a serpentine."

Kate brought Night Owl into the bend of the ring and turned him so he was heading diagonally across to the other side. He did as she asked, but his turn was sharp rather than smooth, and as he crossed the ring she could feel him picking up speed.

When they reached the opposite end of the ring, Kate turned Night Owl again and they went back the way they had come, this time covering the ring in three looping arcs. When she completed the exercise she turned in the saddle to watch Jessie, who was barely through the first of the snakelike curves.

"Are they supposed to be done that quickly?" Jessie asked when she reached Kate. "Jonathan looks like slow motion compared to the Bird."

"No," Kate said glumly. "Jonathan was going the right speed. Night Owl's turned into a sprinter."

"Slow him down," Jessie said.

Kate shook her head. "I *am* trying to slow him down but for some reason the old methods aren't working anymore. I ask him to slow down and he stops."

"What's your mom say?"

"She hasn't seen him at his worst. Can you pick anything out?"

Jessie brushed a lock of brown hair from her brow and chewed her lip. "You look a little stiff. Not as loose as usual. Not relaxed."

"I am a little stiff," Kate said, her voice sharpening. "But it's because Night Owl is acting like such a dork."

"He'll be all right," Jessie said, soothing her friend. "You've got weeks before the show."

Kate wondered how the word weeks could sometimes sound like all the time in the world, and sometimes like no time at all. "Jonathan's looking good," Kate said, changing the subject. "Too bad *he's* not going to be showing this year."

"Yeah." Jessie's eyes moved away from Kate's. There was a note of sadness in her voice. "If he behaves this way all the time, he might just win a ribbon." She looked back toward the barn.

"What's the matter?" Kate asked, but she already knew what was the matter.

Jessie said, "I'm going to sound ungrateful. It's just Time-Out. I miss her. And it's strange not being in the shows this year."

"I know," Kate said. "If only ..."

Suddenly, Jessie grinned. "Enough of this. Hey, here we are on a beautiful day, riding beautiful horses, and complaining."

"You're right. No more complaints, no looking back," Kate said, with more confidence than she felt. She gave Night Owl a squeeze and started him moving. "You can help, too," she told him, "by not giving me stuff to complain about."

Chapter 5

IT was a good thing Kate had Home Ec first period because her mind was definitely not on schoolwork. It was on Pete Hastings. Ever since he'd offered to wait with her in the cafeteria last week, she'd had the feeling that he was paying more attention to her than usual. Then last night, just before she'd gone to bed, he'd called. He hadn't even made up an excuse, such as asking her for the math assignment. He'd just called and talked. For a long time. For almost as long as she and Jessie talked.

Then this morning on the bus, instead of sitting behind her and leaning over her shoulder, he'd sat next to her.

"You're awfully quiet this morning," Jessie said to Kate in Home Ec. She washed the last mixing bowl and handed it to Kate to dry.

"I was thinking," Kate said.

"What about?" Jessie emptied the sink and sprinkled it with cleanser.

"Pete Hastings called me last night."

"Oh-oh," Jessie said, making her eyes wide and humming the theme from "The Twilight Zone."

"What's that supposed to mean?" Kate asked.

"I think he likes you."

"Why?"

Jessie pretended to think about that, then said, "It must be your money. It can't be your personality or your looks."

Kate swatted her with a towel. "I mean why now? I've known him for half my life."

"So what did he say?"

"Nothing special. We just talked. And then this morning he sat next to me on the bus."

"I bet he asks you out," Jessie said. "He's cute."

"He is, isn't he?" Kate said.

English was Kate's next class, and she was having trouble paying attention. Plus, she still hadn't handed the book report in, and now it was really late. It seemed to Kate that her head was too small to hold all the worries she was carrying around. She had them sectioned off. There were school worries, and horse worries and now, there were Pete worries.

Something inside her jittered and flip-flopped when she thought of Pete. What would it be like to go out on a date? Pete was driving; he'd gotten his license two months ago. That was one of the

things he told her last night. She pictured them
going to the movies, maybe out for pizza first. She
wondered if he'd expect her to get all dressed up?
That made her even more jittery—she didn't own
a dress, not one. And with a new pair of riding
boots on the agenda, she probably wouldn't get a
dress very soon ...

"And that kind of a rhyme pattern is called?
Kate, suppose you tell us."

Kate came back to the classroom with a start
and looked blankly at Mrs. Rottman. What in the
world had the class been talking about?

"Iambic pentameter," Amory whispered from
directly behind her. She repeated the words out
loud, Mrs. Rottman nodded and went on with the
lesson.

Kate turned a little sideways in her seat so she
could thank Amory, then forced herself to empty
her mind of everything but English.

At lunch Kate bought herself a carton of milk
and sat down to eat the fresh bread they'd made
that morning in Home Ec.

"If you give me a piece of that, I'll let you eat
some of my extra shelving from shop class."

Kate looked up to see Pete standing next to
her. She smiled, but there was a little knot of
anxiety, not really an unpleasant feeling, in her
stomach. She handed him half a roll and said he
could eat her part of the shelving himself.

"Great!" he said. "There's nothing like some

knotty pine at two o'clock in the afternoon to cut down on those empty-stomach blues."

Monica arrived and plunked herself down. "What a morning," she wailed. "I broke three nails in typing."

"I have news for you," Pete said, leaning across Kate, "they grow back."

"Oh don't be so funny. These don't. They cost me thirty-five dollars at the mall."

Kate shook her head and looked at her own nails, cut almost to the quick. "Well that's one expense I don't have," she said.

"What's for lunch today?" Pete looked over at Monica's tray, overflowing with kinds of food other than her usual dish of greens.

"I'm not sure," Monica said, looking at her plate. "They had this white stuff." She poked her fork into a mound on her plate. "And then they had this brown stuff." She poked at another mound.

Jessie slipped into the empty seat next to Kate. "How come you're eating?" she asked Monica.

"Because I'm depressed. Besides, the salads looked crummy."

"How come you're depressed?" Jessie asked, taking a bite of her sandwich.

"Because she broke a nail," Pete said.

Monica said nothing.

Amory wandered up to the table, his glasses riding halfway down his nose, his brown hair flopping over his forehead. He was probably the smartest boy Kate knew. She thanked him again for saving her life in English. "No sweat," Amory said.

"Charming way to put it," Monica muttered.

"Where's Bruce?" Pete asked Amory.

"I saw him talking to Gloria Skinner."

Pete whistled. "That's big time."

"And that's what's wrong with Monica," Jessie whispered to Kate. "She's got a crush on him."

Just then Kristin and Bruce arrived. Kristin was a short, plump girl, with shining red hair and big brown eyes. She was the most laid-back person Kate had ever met. Nothing in the world seemed to bother her. "So listen, you guys," she said. "Local Streets is giving a concert in Hartford on Saturday and my brother can get tickets. Anybody want to go?"

"We all want to go," Amory said, "but I for one can't afford it."

"How about you?" Kristin said to Pete.

"I could probably scrape the bucks together. Do you want to go?" he looked at Kate.

She blushed and hated herself for it. "I—I can't," she stammered. "I have a show coming up in a few weeks."

"But the concert is Saturday *night*," Kristin said.

"I still don't have time."

"You're going to be tied up every minute between now and the end of the month?" Pete asked. She could tell by his voice he didn't believe her.

"Almost." She felt under attack.

"That's ridiculous," Bruce said. "Even the football team doesn't practice that much. And football's a lot harder than riding a horse."

"It is not," Jessie said. "In the first place, you have to ..." She paused and looked at Kate.

"You have to have a horse," Bruce put in.

Monica laughed.

"Cool it, Bruce," Pete said. "I'd really like to know. To tell you the truth, it doesn't look like all that much work."

"I'd like to see one of you guys do what Kate does," Jessie said, looking from Bruce to Pete.

"But what *does* she do?" Monica and Bruce asked at the same time.

Jessie sighed. "Look, my explaining it to you isn't going to do any good. Why don't you come to the show at The Hill? It's not that far away. Then, after you've seen Kate ride, you tell me if you still think you can do what she does."

"Jessie!" Kate said. She was already nervous enough without having half the sophomore class watching her.

"Kate's probably the best rider in all of Connecticut," Jessie went on, ignoring Kate. "Jessie," Kate said, putting her hand over her friend's mouth, "shut up!"

"She is?" Bruce gave Kate a measured look. "Okay, then I think we should all go and check out this horse-showing thing. All in favor raise your hand." Monica's hand flew up immediately. "How about you, Pete, you gonna check it out?"

"For sure," he said, and gave Kate one of those

fantastic smiles. "But I don't want to get you mad."

"You won't get her mad," Jessie said, ignoring the daggers Kate was sending her way. "I think you're going to be very impressed."

"Thanks loads," Kate whispered to Jessie under her breath. "Remind me to do you a favor sometime."

Chapter 6

KATE walked up the driveway slowly, banging the morning's copy of the *Connecticut Horseman* against her leg. Her mood was as gray as the day.

Miss Molly and two other boarders were in the near field. They heard her coming and three heads came up to stare at her. Miss Molly neighed loudly, arched her tail and galloped across the field as if Kate were someone to be scared of. The other horses hesitated a moment, then joined her. "Molly, you are wacky," Kate said.

She entered the house through the front door, instead of walking around to the back, dropped her books on the hall table, and headed for the kitchen.

Today, her mother absolutely had to take the time to work with her no matter what. For the last week, anytime Mrs. Wiley wandered by the ring when Kate and Jessie were riding, she'd stop to watch a minute and call encouragement or correction. But today she *had* to drop everything else and give Kate her full attention. The first show of the season was just over a week away.

"Is that you, Kate?" her mother called from the den.

"What are you doing in here?" Kate looked in to see her mother sitting at the desk, writing.

"I just got another call from the stable in Pennsylvania. They're shipping that new horse tonight. They figure he'll get here about eight."

"Tonight? Why so fast? Who's the owner?"

"Koppel?" Anne said, looking down at the name on her pad. "That doesn't sound right, but that's what it looks like. I never did learn to write and talk on the phone at the same time. And I don't know why the rush."

"Swell," Kate said, sitting down dejectedly on the couch.

"Hey, this is good news," Anne Wiley said.

"It would be if I wasn't trying so hard to get some time with you. I don't suppose you'd be willing to call the owners and have them come over to get things ready for their horse so that you and I could spend some time in the ring?"

Mrs. Wiley made a face. "The owners aren't around to call. They won't be moving up until later. I'm afraid there isn't anyone to call."

"That's not fair," Kate said.

"You're in a prickly mood," her mother said. "And that's not like you."

"Well, I haven't had a very good day."

"Tell me."

"First, I still haven't handed in that book report, and now it's so late, no matter how hard I work on it I can't get more than a C."

"That's better than an F," her mother said. When Kate didn't respond, she said, "What else?"

"Night Owl's still being a real pain. I keep telling you that, and you don't seem to believe it."

"Whatever's gone wrong between you and Night Owl can't take all that much to fix."

"Yeah, but you've got to spend some time with me to fix it," Kate said morosely.

"What else is wrong?" her mother asked quietly.

"Jessie invited the whole gang from school to see me ride at The Hill."

"Don't you want them to come?"

"No."

"Why not? They're your friends."

"Jessie told them I was the best rider in the state of Connecticut."

"Kate," her mother said, "you're getting yourself all worked up over nothing."

"Nothing?" Kate said, amazed. "I'm tired of hearing what a great rider I am. Last year I almost believed it. But this year? The way things are going with Night Owl? I'll be lucky if they don't excuse me from competition." She felt close to tears.

It would be bad enough to make a poor showing in front of all her horse-show friends, but at least she didn't have to see them every day of her life. She could just imagine what Pete would think of her if she didn't come home with the blue ribbon after all Jessie's bragging.

"You really are upset." Kate's mother sat next to her on the couch and put an arm around her shoulder. "I'm sorry. Look, you go change your clothes and we'll spend as much time in the ring as you need."

"What about the new horse?" Kate swallowed hard to keep her voice steady.

"First your problems, my sweet, then the new horse's problems. What's the worst that can happen? His stall won't be ready in time and he'll have to spend the night in the field. Is it a deal?"

"It's a deal," Kate said, rubbing her hands over her teary eyes. "I feel like a dope for getting so worked up."

"You can feel dopey around your mother, it's allowed," Anne said and laughed. "Now go change your clothes and get down to the barn. We have work to do."

The day had turned chilly and a brisk wind was blowing. Kate trotted Night Owl around the ring to warm him up. She could see her mother rubbing her arms to chase away the cold.

"Okay, Katie May," her mother called, "give me a twenty-meter circle."

Kate brought Night Owl down alongside the rail, then turned him so that he was circling in half the ring.

"Bring him forward, Kate. He's going on his forehand like a hunter, gather him up."

Kate adjusted her hold, shortening the reins a little, and Night Owl made contact with the bit. The big bay's head tucked in and his stride shortened.

"Better, that's better, get those hindquarters driving. Good. One–two, one–two," her mother counted out the rhythm of the trot. "Keep it nice and even, slow him down."

"Do you think he's bending any?" Kate asked.

"Not much," her mother said. "Forget that for now, I'll give you an exercise to do, to see if we can supple him up some. Okay, straight along the rail. Straight. Don't let him waver, and get your leg behind the cinch—your outside leg, he's swinging his rear end out."

For the better part of an hour, Kate worked with her mother, and with every minute that went by, she could feel herself relaxing. Night Owl, who started the lesson with all his current bad habits in place, got better and better, and by the end of the lesson he was going very well.

"What's so terrible about him?" her mother asked when they were taking a break.

Kate smiled with the first real happiness she'd felt in days. "Nothing today. He went nicely. See? I told you I needed you. An hour with you and we're stars again."

"Keep him walking while I set these up." Anne took a stack of highway cones painted with letters and placed them at precise points around the ring. "Let's give the first test a quick run through."

"I haven't memorized it yet," Kate protested.

"I'll read it to you," Anne said, digging a copy of the schedule out of her jacket pocket.

Kate took Night Owl between the two cones that marked the entrance. "Enter, working trot," Anne called out. "Halt and salute." Night Owl trotted to the center of the ring and stopped. Kate bowed her head in the direction where the judges should be sitting. "Proceed, working trot, at letter C, trace right."

They went through the entire test and when they were finished, Night Owl stood motionless in the center of the ring. Again Kate bowed to the imaginary judges, then turned quickly to look at her mother.

Anne's face was bright with her smile. "That was very good."

"Yeah," Kate said, delighted. "I could feel it, too."

"Just watch your half-halts. If we can get him to bend a little more, you'll be home free. Actually," she said, and smiled, "I think you both could learn to bend a little more."

"If I bend any more, I'll snap," Kate said, and sighed wearily.

"That might be part of the problem. If you're tight enough to snap, you're not loose enough to bend."

"It's just that the dressage score is so important," Kate said. "Night Owl may be a great jumper, but it won't matter if we blow the dressage. What's the exercise you were going to give me to help him bend in the corners? Maybe I can do it, too." She grinned.

"It involves cantering in a spiral around some jump standards," her mother said, and laughed. "You still think you want to try it?"

"Maybe I'll opt for a hot bath," Kate said.

"A much better idea. No more today. Tomorrow I'll explain the exercise and set up the standards for you. And I promise to find some time every day to watch you ride. But right now I'm freezing and there's still all that stuff to be done before the new horse gets here. I'm going to run into the house to put on something warmer. I'll be right out."

"I'll cool him down and see you in the barn," Kate said. She gave Night Owl a loose rein and let him saunter around the ring. She patted his neck. "You were so good," she crooned, her voice warm with relief. "Just see that you stay that way."

Kate put a light blanket over Night Owl and left him in the paddock while she cleaned his stall. She was nearly finished when Jessie arrived. "Kate," Jessie said from the doorway, "is your mom here?" There was a funny note in her voice.

"No," Kate said, straightening up to face her. "She's in the house. Why?"

"I was coming down the driveway and I thought I heard somebody calling for help from your house."

Kate dropped the pitchfork and started for the door. "Are you sure you heard *help*?" she asked.

"It was kind of faint, but that's what it sounded like to me."

By the time she reached the driveway, Kate was running. She was at the kitchen door when she heard it—her mother's voice. She raced through the entryway and into the kitchen. "Kate," her mother called weakly, "is that you?"

"Where are you?" Kate cried. Fear made her heart pound.

"In the basement."

Kate dashed to the basement stairs and there, sitting in the middle of the flight of steps, was her mother, a half-empty basket of apples on her lap.

"What's the matter?" Kate asked, hurrying toward her.

"I've twisted my knee again." Anne's voice was tight with pain. "It hurts worse than it ever has."

Kate tried to keep her voice calm. "Don't move, Mom. Jessie and I will help you."

The girls supported Mrs. Wiley until they had her on the couch in the den. "Look at that," she said, gingerly pulling up the leg of her sweat pants. Her knee was swollen to twice its normal size. "That accident I had may have happened years ago, but it certainly keeps coming back to haunt me."

"I better call the doctor," Kate said.

Her mother shut her eyes against the pain. "Don't bother, the doctor always says the same thing: Stay off it until two days after the swelling goes down."

"Last time it took a week," Kate said, "and it didn't look anywhere near as bad as it does now. What happened? Did you fall down the stairs?"

"No." Her mother attempted a smile. "If I had, at least there'd have been some drama in it. I fell *up* the stairs. I went down to get the last of the apples and coming back I just slipped—big thump, apples all over the place and me a cripple again." Her eyes reddened and she banged the arm of the sofa with her fist. "Damn, there's so much to do."

"Don't worry, Mom. We can handle things," Kate assured her.

"I know you'll try, honey. It's just that being laid up is such a pain in the neck."

"In the knee," Jessie said softly, and Anne smiled tightly. "Right, I almost forgot." Anne grimaced. "The new horse!"

"A new horse?" Jessie said with interest.

"We'll handle that, too," Kate said, but she couldn't help wondering how. "When will Dad be home?"

"Soon. He had another meeting with those new clients. But when he gets home he's going to have to load me in the car and take me to the clinic."

"Here." Kate offered her mother an afghan. "Stay still and get well. That's an order. I need you back on your feet by next weekend."

"The show." Anne moaned. "You'd better not count on me being there."

Katie looked at her in amazement. Not count on

her being there? That was ridiculous. She did count on it. Not only did Kate need her at the show, she needed her in the practice ring, tomorrow and the day after that, and the day after that. She was about to say all that when she realized how pale her mother looked. "It's bad, isn't it?" she said with concern.

"It'll pass," her mother replied. "Just as long as I don't move. The horses haven't even been fed," she said, and to Kate's dismay, there were tears in her eyes. "Do that before you get the new stall ready."

"Don't worry about a thing. Jessie and I'll handle it all."

"Sure, Mrs. Wiley," Jessie added. "We can do it. Who's the new stall for?"

"And you're going to have to reorganize the tack room," Anne went on.

Kate sighed, thinking of the hours of work ahead of her, then turned quickly to Jessie. "Jessie, could you possibly stay and help me get everything done?"

"Only if somebody will tell me about that new horse," Jessie said, exasperated.

Mrs. Wiley gave a small laugh and told Jessie about the call from Pennsylvania.

"Thank you," Jessie said to Mrs. Wiley, then turned to Kate. "Of course I'll stay, just let me call Mrs. Quincy."

"Is that the new housekeeper?" Mrs. Wiley asked. "How is she working out?"

"I like her a lot," Jessie said. "I just hope Nicholas and Sarah behave themselves so she'll stay a while." Jessie made a quick telephone call and came back to say that she was Kate's for the evening.

"You two are wonderful," Mrs. Wiley said softly. "Have I told you that today? Come here and let me give both of you a big hug."

By seven o'clock the barn was dark and cozy. Kate and Jessie sat at the table in the tack room, school books spread out in front of them, doing their homework.

Jessie looked up from her books. "I like it here with the horses," she said. "Remember last year, when we used to do this all the time? And the year before that, right before the first shows? When we practically lived out here?" She was quiet for a minute, remembering happier days. "Do you know anything about this new horse?" she asked, closing her math book and reaching for her English text.

"No, just what I've said."

"I think it's neat that they were told this was the best facility in the area," Jessie said. "Who sent them here?"

"We were wondering that, too. Maybe the owners will tell us, if they ever show up."

At that moment they heard the sound of an engine, a heavy truck motor. The sound of tires in the drive made them both leap up.

They bounded outside, pulling their sweaters around them. Two large headlights swung in an arc lighting up the swaying sign that said Windcroft Stables, and a heavy truck lumbered into the driveway. Kate walked toward the truck just as her father came out of the house. "Mr. Wiley?" the truck driver called down from his window.

"Yes," Marc answered. "We're expecting you."

The driver opened the door and climbed down slowly. "I've got one gray gelding, seventeen hands, named Arpeggio. That jive with your information?"

"From Concordia Stables in Lancaster, Pennsylvania?"

"Right on," the driver said. "Let's get those ramps in place," he called to his helper.

Kate and Jessie stood to one side and waited. The hollow thud of hooves moving around on the wooden truck bed sounded. Then, framed in the doorway was a large, tense-looking horse. His head was as high as the lead line would allow, his ears were pointed dead forward, and he was sniffing the air.

"Come on, big guy, let's move it," the driver said patiently. Arpeggio stood his ground and looked them over. "I'd think you'd be happy to get out of there." He clucked his tongue and jiggled the lead rope. "Give him a swat from behind, Harry," he called to his assistant. Harry smacked the big gray on his rump, and Arpeggio started down the ramp at a run. "Watch it, here he comes. Whoa, easy does it," the driver said, running a few steps with the horse when he reached the ground. Arpeggio stretched his neck out and shook himself vigorously, then eyed them all suspiciously.

"Oh, look at him," Jessie whispered.

"Where do you want him?" the driver asked.

"Take him over there to that paddock," Kate said, leading the way. "Jessie, turn on the spotlights." With some encouragement from Kate, Arpeggio followed the driver through the gate into the paddock.

The driver unsnapped the lead line and turned the horse loose. "I have some papers here to be signed," he said.

"I'll take care of that. Why don't you come into the barn," Marc Wiley said, leading the way.

The girls stood at the fence and watched Arpeggio circle the small exercise area. His neck was arched, his head high, his nostrils flaring. He pranced in short strides, his forelegs curved and flashing. "He smells the other horses," Kate said. "Arpeggio," she called softly, "how are you?" The horse gave her a brief look and continued his nervous rounds. Halfway across the paddock, he stopped and neighed, a loud ringing sound that immediately quieted all the frogs. From inside the barn, first one horse and then another answered him. Arpeggio neighed again, and pawed the ground.

"He's beautiful," Jessie said. "Who are you going to let out with him to keep him company?"

"Night Owl. He's the easiest to get along with. Watch him and make sure he doesn't decide to do something stupid while I get the Bird."

"If he decides to do something stupid I don't think I have a chance of stopping him." Kate understood what Jessie meant. Arpeggio was probably the most powerful horse she had ever seen.

Inside the barn, the horses who were usually quietly eating or sound asleep at this time of night were all pacing nervously in their stalls. "Guess who came to dinner," Kate said when she got to Night Owl.

He was standing tensely with his hind end toward her, his nose glued to his window, sniffing loudly, trying to get a good whiff of the newcomer. "Come on, I'll introduce you." She clipped a lead line to his halter and led him outside. Arpeggio heard them coming and immediately came to the fence, tail flowing, ears pointed straight ahead. Night Owl stopped and whinnied.

"He's a friend," Kate said. "At least, I hope he is."

Kate urged Night Owl forward and opened the gate to the adjoining paddock, then she unclipped his lead line and let him go. He trotted immediately to the fence that separated him from the gray. Arpeggio came toward him at a stiff-legged trot. They breathed heavily, each horse taking in the breath of the other one. It was the horsey equivalent of a long, searching look and a hearty handshake. Night Owl tossed his head and ran a few steps away, then came back again. The gray was waiting. They shook hands again.

"I think he likes him," Jessie said.

"Yeah," Kate agreed, sighing with relief. "I think

it's going to be all right. Okay, let's get his tack stowed away and find out if he's eaten. We'll leave them out there together for a while and hope we can get Arpeggio into the barn when the time comes."

"He *is* gorgeous," Jessie said.

"That's the third time you've mentioned it," Kate said. He was a spectacular horse, and though she would never say it to another living soul, he might even be better looking than Night Owl. She just wished Jessie would stop pointing it out.

"If you had a horse that looked like that would you just ship him to some place you had never seen before, and not be there when he arrived?" Jessie wondered aloud.

"No," Kate said.

Jessie sighed. "Some people don't know how good they have it."

Chapter 7

THE days passed in a blur for Kate. It seemed to her the entire world was made up of nothing but work. Work and worry, because her mother's knee, instead of getting better, was getting worse.

They had taken Anne to the clinic again when her knee failed to show any improvement, and the doctor had looked at it and shaken his head. "I hate to tell you this, Anne, but it's time to think about surgery."

Her mother had objected strenuously, but her father had agreed with the doctor. "It's more time off your feet now, that's true. But if you don't have the operation, these episodes will get worse."

"I'll think about it," Anne had said. She'd turned to the doctor. "Any chance I can use crutches?"

"None," he'd replied. "I want you absolutely off your feet."

"How long will Mom be in bed if she has the surgery?" Kate asked her father after they'd gotten Anne home again.

"She won't have to stay in bed, but she'll be confined to the house for six weeks or so."

Kate looked at him with her eyes wide. "How can we do without Mom for six weeks? How can *I* do without her?"

"If it comes to an operation, I'll get someone to help with the farm."

But her father didn't understand. It wasn't just the work around the farm that had Kate so upset. It was the training sessions with Night Owl. After that one super practice round with her mother coaching, he had gone right back to being impossible. He was getting more unworkable by the day.

And as the days had passed, another worry was added to Kate's list: Arpeggio. His owner hadn't arrived yet. Without any instructions, Kate hadn't known what to do with him. It was more than a week now that he hadn't been ridden, and for an eventing horse, which Kate suspected he was, that could spell trouble. But without his owner's permission, she wasn't going to get on his back. So he got turned out once a day with Night Owl and Jonathan. They played together, and that was the sum total of his exercise.

On the Monday after the big Local Streets concert, Kate threaded her way through the crowded cafeteria to her lunch table. Neither Pete nor

Monica had been on the bus. She wondered if Pete had driven Monica to school. Maybe Monica had switched her crush from Bruce to Pete, a thought that didn't make Kate happy.

She stopped short as she neared her table. There was an unfamiliar girl sitting in what should have been Kate's seat. Jessie, seeing what had happened, got up and pulled a chair from the next table for Kate to sit in.

"Who's that?" Kate whispered as she sat down.

"She's new," Jessie said. "Her name is Dara. That's all I know."

She's sitting in my seat! Kate wanted to say, and for some reason the words made her feel like crying.

The girl was deep in conversation with Bruce Davidson, and Pete was kind of hanging over her shoulder, listening. She was very pretty. Pretty wasn't quite the word, Kate decided. Gorgeous was more like it. She had blond hair, darker than Kate's and shorter. It wasn't curly or set-looking, but Kate could tell just from the way it fell that somebody very good had cut it. It looked like a cut from *Seventeen* magazine. Her bangs were long and full and stopped just short of amazingly blue eyes. She had a nose that turned up a bit, and a wide, full-lipped mouth.

"I know," Dara was saying to Bruce in a deep, throaty voice. "That happens to me, too." And they laughed. "Well, not *exactly* the same way it happens to you," she said and they laughed again. This time Pete joined them.

Even Amory, with his serious face and his dislike of small talk, was hanging on every word she said.

"Didn't take her long to make friends," Monica muttered. Monica hated being upstaged.

Pete and Bruce finished whatever it was they were saying and went back to eating.

The new girl looked up at Kate and smiled. "Hi."

"Kate, meet Dara; Dara, meet Kate," Jessie said.

"Kate will say hello as soon as she stops chewing," Bruce obligingly pointed out.

Kate swallowed and managed a smile, wondering if murdering Bruce was a punishable offense. "Hi," she said.

"So how long have you been in town?" Monica said. "That is, if you're finished talking to the boys." Her last words were little barbs aimed at Bruce.

"I don't know," Dara said, her husky voice stopping just short of a drawl. "Are we finished talking?" She looked from Bruce to Pete.

"For now," Pete said with a grin.

For the first time in her life, Kate lost her appetite.

"Where's your next class?" Monica asked brightly.

"Room three-oh-seven," Dara answered, "but Pete and Bruce said they'd show me where it was."

"I thought you guys had gym after lunch," Monica said.

"We do," Bruce said, "but her history room's right on the way."

"It is not . . ." Monica started to say, but Kate kicked her under the table. "Well, it's *not*," Monica said in an angry hiss to Kate. "Whose idea was it to ask her to eat with us?" she asked, still in a whisper. The girls looked across at Dara, who was deep in conversation with Bruce and Pete again.

"Oh, Monica, don't be that way. She's new in school. You know how hard that can be," Kristin whispered, then added wistfully, "She can't help it if she's gorgeous."

"Okay, don't take it seriously. But more dates are arranged over the lunch table than anyplace else in this school. I took a poll."

"You did?" Kate asked, looking at her in amazement.

"Yes," Monica said, standing up, "and I wish you'd wake up to the fact that there's more to life than *horses*." She picked up her tray and stalked off.

"I'll go and calm her down," Kristin said, and hurried after Monica.

"Horses?" Dara asked, breaking away from her conversation with Pete and Bruce. "Did I hear somebody say horses?"

Before either Kate or Jessie could answer her, Douglas Lyons pushed his way through the crowded room to their table. He pulled out Monica's empty chair and sat down. Jessie grabbed Kate's arm so tightly, Kate thought her circulation had been cut off. Doug Lyons was probably the best-looking boy in the entire school, president of the junior class and co-captain of the football team.

"Monica will die that she missed him," Jessie whispered to Kate. "We'll have to get her chair bronzed."

"Are you Dara Cooper?" he asked.

"Yes," Dara said in her clipped, finishing-school accent. "Are you Doug Lyons?"

"That's me. Welcome to Smithfield Regional High School."

"I went to school with Doug's cousin in Pennsylvania. I used to live in Lancaster," she explained to the other kids at the table. "I was hoping I'd run into you. I've got a message for you from Greg."

"He told me to keep my eye out for you. But right now I have a class meeting that I'm late for. How about if I meet you after school?"

"That'd be fine," Dara said.

"Good. I'll meet you at the gym entrance," Doug said, and left, moving lightly through the crowd, dodging people the way he did players in a football game.

"Except," Dara said, "I don't know where the gym entrance is."

The boys offered to show her at once. It seemed to Kate that they almost tripped over each other as they stood, with Dara between them. "See ya," Pete waved to Kate and Jessie. Dara waved too, and they left.

"Well," Jessie said, watching them go, "all I can

say is, I'm glad I'm not counting on a date for Spring Fling. I'd hate to have to compete with Dara for attention."

"I'm too busy to worry about dances," Kate said, hoping the words sounded more truthful than they were.

"Sure," Jessie said.

"I *am*. And you know that better than anyone, Jessie."

"Okay." Jessie held up both hands. "You're too busy. Even too busy for a date with Pete. I understand."

Kate felt herself blushing, and quickly changed the subject. "I wish you could get out early today, so we could get our riding in before I start doing the chores."

Jessie stopped in her tracks and slapped the heel of her hand against her forehead. "Oh no, I almost forgot. Kate, I can't come today."

"Why not?"

"The new housekeeper. She quit. Said she couldn't handle Nicholas. Dad's interviewing another one tonight. But for today, *I'm* the house-keeper."

"Oh, great," Kate moaned. "I need you, Jessie. I need your help when I'm working Night Owl."

"Don't worry." Jessie squeezed her hand. "I'll be there tomorrow, and all weekend. Even if I have to bring Sarah and Nicholas along."

Later, when she and Jessie parted company at their lockers, Kate saw Pete coming down the hall toward her. "Hi," he said, falling into step beside her.

"Where's Dara?" Kate asked, surprised to hear the sharpness in her voice.

"We took her up to the third floor, where her next class is."

"It must have been hard to tear yourself away."

"What's with you these days?" Pete asked, his brown eyes serious.

Kate shrugged and felt herself blushing again. She hadn't meant to sound so jealous—she hadn't even known she *was* jealous.

They walked a few steps in silence. "You're going to like Dara when you get to know her," Pete said quietly. "She's into horses, too. She was asking about you. I told her about your eventing and that your parents run a stable."

"And was she thrilled?"

"What's that supposed to mean?" Pete asked, and frowned.

Kate turned away from him, knowing she was acting like a three year old, but she didn't seem able to help it.

"I told her we were all going to see you compete at The Hill," Pete went on cautiously, as if he wasn't sure anymore how Kate would react.

Kate stopped walking and turned to face Pete. "You didn't invite her to come. Did you?"

"No. But this is the part I thought you'd be interested in. She's going to be showing at The Hill, too."

"She isn't," Kate gasped.

"See," Pete said, "I knew you'd be surprised. Well, I have to run. I'll try to call you, maybe tonight."

Kate watched him leave. Another wonderful surprise. Almost as terrific as her mother being laid up with a bad knee. Dara Cooper, poised and beautiful, would be showing at The Hill, too.

"I don't need this." Kate moaned aloud. "Why didn't Dara just stay in Lancaster, Pennsylvania, where she belongs?"

Lancaster, Pennsylvania. Kate stopped dead in her tracks. That's where Arpeggio is from.

You could be wrong, she said to herself hopefully, but she knew that was too much to ask. Arpeggio belonged to Dara; she'd bet her last dollar on it.

Dara *and* Arpeggio *and* the whole gang from school at The Hill.

Chapter 8

WHY was she always right when she wanted most desperately to be wrong? Kate tightly held Miss Molly's bridle and watched the silver Mercedes-Benz pull into the driveway. A small woman with a head of wildly curly hair got out of the driver's seat, and Dara Cooper got out on the passenger's side. They started toward the house, then saw Kate. The two of them came walking toward the paddock.

Dara smiled when she saw her. "Hi," she said. "It's Kate, isn't it? Kate Wiley?"

"Yes," Kate answered, walking Molly over to the fence. "I guess you belong to Arpeggio."

"Is he all right?" Mrs. Cooper asked.

"Yes," Kate said, "He's fine." Then couldn't help adding, "It's always hard for a horse to get settled in a new place, especially if there's nobody around he knows. But we did the best we could."

Dara was looking at Kate with a lazy kind of smile that struck Kate as vaguely condescending. "He's a big boy," she said. "He doesn't get upset over changes."

"I hope your best is good enough," Mrs. Cooper said crisply. She looked around, taking in the barn and the outside ring. "I have to say, this isn't at all what I expected. Do you have an indoor ring?"

"Almost." Kate fought down a feeling of dislike for the woman.

"Dara," Mrs. Cooper said, "I'm not entirely sure that this will work out, after all."

"Could we see Arpeggio?" Dara asked, ignoring her mother.

Kate shrugged and led them into the barn.

"He *is* handsome, isn't he?" Dara said to her mother when they had reached Arpeggio's stall. "When I haven't seen him for a while, I forget."

"He'd better be," Mrs. Cooper replied, dusting her hands off. "He certainly cost enough. Call me when you want to come home." Mrs. Cooper picked her way out gingerly, stopping to brush a piece of hay from her coat. She paused to look into the tack room, shook her head, and left.

Dara unlocked the stall and walked in with her horse. He studied her calmly as she ran a hand over his shoulders and down his legs, then across his back. "You're in fine shape," she told him.

"All our horses are," Kate said stiffly. "I put your tack in with our stuff," she added, pointing toward the tack room. "You may want to store it yourself ... someplace else."

Dara looked as if she were going to say something, then changed her mind. "Thanks. I appreciate the fact that you had to take care of him for us. It was just such a hassle getting everything up here. My mother insisted on having the Marone Brothers move him, and they had only that one day when a van was available. Otherwise we'd have had to wait for a month."

"They mustn't move horses around a lot in Pennsylvania. We can get a van anytime up here."

"We could in Pennsylvania, too, if my mother would use someone besides the Marone Brothers. They're the 'in' people to move your horse."

"You're kidding," Kate said.

Dara shrugged. "I thought it was dumb, too. But Mother's into the 'in' things. Like my trainer in Lancaster. He was *very* 'in.'"

Kate thought, Oh, spare me! But she managed a weak smile and said, "So who told you about us?"

"My trainer. He knows someone in the area. Pietro Yon. Do you know him? I'm hoping to get him as my coach."

Of course, Kate thought. Pietro Yon was probably considered *very* "in." "He's a good friend of my family."

"Is he your coach?"

"No. My mother coaches me."

"Your mother?" Dara's eyebrows shot up. Then she laughed.

"My mother is very good," Kate said, too defensively.

"I'm sorry," Dara said. "That isn't why I was

laughing. I was just picturing *my* mother coaching me." She laughed again and shook her head. "You must be on very good terms with your mother."

"I am," Kate said. "She's taught me everything I know."

"Then you're lucky. It must be wonderful to have your family as interested in horses as you are."

"Isn't your family interested?"

"Only in whether or not I win," Dara said, stroking Arpeggio again. "Does your mother work out with you every day?"

"Usually. She's laid up at the moment, though. She has a knee problem. That's why she's not out here to meet you. So there's a lot more barn work to do than usual, and my time is kind of scrunched."

"Maybe we can ride together." Dara examined Arpeggio's legs while she spoke, making the suggestion sound unimportant. "Have you ridden today?"

"Yes," Kate said quickly. Since Jessie wasn't going to show today, Kate had tacked up and ridden early. "I ride Night Owl first thing," she said, "as soon as I get home from school. I have early dismissal." She kept her voice cool. She wanted no hint of an invitation in it.

"Can I see your horse?" Dara asked.

Kate led the way to his stall, and Night Owl came to the bars, nickering softly, blowing at Kate. "Hi, sweetie," she said. His large eyes looked at her and then shifted to Dara. "This is Arpeggio's mom," Kate said, and to Dara: "They're good friends. We've been turning them out together."

"He's nice," Dara said.

It was true, and Kate wondered why the words bothered her. Night Owl *was* nice, in many wonderful ways. Arpeggio, on the other hand, was spectacular.

"Well, I've got a lot to do," Kate said. "I don't think you'll have any trouble finding what you need. Things are pretty straightforward here. I'll be mucking stalls if you need me."

"Thanks," Dara said. Kate thought she heard a touch of disappointment in her voice. But she put it out of her mind. She was not going to worry about one more thing, or one more person, least of all Dara Cooper.

Kate worked quietly in the farthest reaches of the barn until she was sure Dara had tacked up and moved outside. Then she went into the tack room where she could look out the window and not be seen.

Dara and Arpeggio were working in the outdoor ring, trotting, doing large circles, then smaller ones. They moved into figure eights and finally serpentines. They did them well; Dara was relaxed and in control. They did them so well that Kate turned around to face the dark wall of the tack room so she wouldn't have to watch them anymore.

"Who was that in the Mercedes-Benz?" her mother asked when Kate came in for dinner.

"The Coopers," Kate said. "Arpeggio's owners."

"That's what I thought. What were they like? I hate not being out there to meet new owners."

Kate walked to the sink and washed her hands, then got herself a glass of water. "They were nice," she said noncommittally.

"The girl looks about your age."

"She is," Kate said. "I met her in school today."

"She looked good in the ring," Anne Wiley said. "I was watching."

"She is good." Kate dried her hands.

"This may work out very well," Anne said. "I know you have Jessie for company, but it pays to ride with someone whose skills are as polished as the Cooper girl's."

Kate looked at her mother sharply. What was she trying to say? That Dara was a better rider than she was and maybe some if it would rub off on her? "Maybe," Kate said, facing away from her mother. "But I like to ride as soon as I get here. Dara doesn't come until late."

"But you always wait for Jessie," Anne said.

"Today I couldn't wait."

Her mother watched her down the glass of water, then said thoughtfully, "You've been awfully touchy lately, Kate. If things are getting to be too much for you, we can hire someone."

"I'm all right." Kate forced some conviction into her words. She knew very well that the stable was barely breaking even. There was no money left over for luxuries like hired help. "I had a rough day at school, that's all. By the way," she

said, changing the subject. "It was Mr. Yon who
told Arpeggio's trainer about Windcroft. Dara says
she's going to try and get him for a coach."

"Did he really?" Anne said, smiling. "I'll have to
call and thank him."

Kate was on the verge of saying it might be
safer to wait until Mrs. Cooper decided if the
accommodations were "in" enough to suit her,
but her mother's smile was so happy, she just
couldn't.

"Did you tell her that Mr. Yon is retiring?" Anne
asked.

Kate shook her head. "Why don't I just let her
find out from Mr. Yon?"

"Because it would be friendlier to tell her."

"If I see her in school tomorrow, I will," Kate
said, and went upstairs to shower.

They were finished with dinner, and her parents were lingering over a last cup of coffee. Kate
said, "I'll do the night check." She tried to make
the words light as if the chore were nothing,
though every bone in her body ached.

She let herself out the back door. The sky was
steel gray, and the barn was a black silhouette
against it. There was a light on inside, and Kate
thought with annoyance that Dara had forgotten
to turn it out. Just as she got to the edge of the
front lawn, the silver Mercedes turned into the
drive. Kate waited. She had no desire to run into
Mrs. Cooper and Dara again. The light went off in
the barn, and Dara came running out, climbed in
the car, and was gone.

Kate went into the dark barn and stood a moment. She could hear the horses moving quietly. Flicking on the light, she started down the long row of stalls to collect the feed buckets and line them up for the morning. Then she stopped in amazement: In stall after stall the straps that held the buckets were empty and a fresh forkful of hay had been left where the buckets had been. All of the water troughs were filled.

She walked quickly back to the tack room. The buckets were lined up neatly. Each one contained the morning's share of feed, exactly according to the schedules posted at each stall. For a wild moment she thought Jessie had come—it was the kind of thing Jessie used to do for them.

She ran back into the barn and called her. Night Owl whinnied but otherwise it was quiet. She walked slowly back to the house.

Her mom and dad were still sitting at the table finishing their coffee.

"Hey," her father said, "you're back fast."

"Everything was already done," Kate said.

"Gremlins?" her father asked, and smiled.

"I think it was Dara Cooper," she said quietly.

Marc Wiley frowned. "She's paying full board. She doesn't have to do chores."

"I know," Kate said.

"That was very nice of her," Anne Wiley said.

"I know," Kate said again, puzzled.

Upstairs in her room, Kate sat at her desk untwining her long braid and thinking about Dara.

She wasn't like anybody Kate had ever met. She seemed awfully sure of herself, and somehow older than sixteen. She hoped her mother didn't expect them to be friends, because Kate couldn't ever see that happening.

She reached for her books, and realized she had left them on the hall table. Wearily, she got up and padded downstairs in her socks. At the foot of the stairs she could hear her mother just ending a conversation on the telephone. She had been talking to Pietro, Kate realized, because she said to Kate's dad, "He did send the Coopers, God bless him."

"How big a blessing the Coopers are remains to be seen," Kate muttered to herself as she picked up her schoolbooks and turned back to the stairs. But her mother's next comment stopped her.

"He says there are three more of his boarders who are interested in moving here when he closes up."

"No kidding," her dad said. "That means we'll be full. We'll actually start making a profit."

"Unfortunately," Anne continued, "Pietro was going to send them down to take a couple of lessons from me before they decided whether to move or not, but with my knee the way it is, he says it would be better for them not to come. People aren't too keen about having their horses someplace where the person in charge is off her feet. So he's sending them to The Hill to watch Kate. He says he told them that the best way to judge a trainer is to watch her students."

"That's true," Marc Wiley agreed. "Kate's the best advertisement we have."

There was a long silence, then her mother reached out for her father's hand. "I'm going to have that operation, Marc. I can't see any way around it."

Her father's voice was gentle when he answered. "I thought you should, right from the beginning. And the sooner the better."

Kate's stomach did a flip-flop. If her mother went into the hospital, there was no chance at all that she'd even make it to the show, let alone be able to coach Kate before then. And how could her mother let Mr. Yon send someone to watch Kate compete as an advertisement for the stable? It was bad enough that Kate was worried about her own reputation when she showed; how she'd have to be responsible for her mother's, too. For the whole farm's! It wasn't fair! They expected her to save the place single-handedly!

She dragged herself back to her room, spread the books out in front of her, and started to cry.

Chapter 9

THE next day Kate hurried home from school to work out with Night Owl. If she'd ever been more tense and upset, she couldn't remember it. Nothing was going right.

She tried not to think about things as she tacked up Night Owl and led him out into the ring. But the worries wouldn't disappear.

The fact was, Kate was a hundred percent on her own now. Her mom was going into the hospital tomorrow afternoon. Jessie wasn't sure if she could make it today. And then Pete had been hanging all over Dara at school again. Well, so had Bruce and a lot of other guys, too—but that didn't make it any better. And that book report was still hanging over her head. At least she'd found in the library a nice short book that Kristin had suggested—*A Sorrow Beyond Dreams*, by Peter Handke. I could write a book with a title like that, she thought.

Night Owl seemed as jittery as she was this afternoon. In fact, he was downright skittish, throwing his head and refusing to keep the right pace. His turns were jerky and clumsy, and no matter what she did, he refused to listen.

Finally, she did the only thing she could—she gave in, let him have his head, and took him out into the field. "At least we don't have to worry about the cross-country competition," she said with a sigh.

Later, as she brushed him down, she heard Jessie's voice calling to her.

"In here," Kate called back.

Jessie, already wearing her riding hat, walked into Night Owl's stall. "I made it," she said. "Dad's got a new housekeeper, so I'm yours." She looked in at Night Owl, and her smile faded. "Oh ... you already rode."

Kate shrugged. "Yeah, I guess you could call it that. But, look, you can still take Jonathan—" She stopped at the sound of a car pulling into the drive. "That must be Princess Di herself," she said, surprised at her own sharp tone.

Jessie giggled. "Nasty, nasty," she said, moving over to Jonathan's stall. "Well, you're right. I can still get a little riding in today. Unless you need help with the chores."

Dara appeared at that moment, her thick hair brushed back away from her face and held with a gold clip at the nape of her neck. She was wearing spotless light tan breeches and an expensive leather jacket.

"Hi," Dara said, and looked over at Jessie in surprise. "Oh, I didn't realize that you rode, too. Is that your horse?"

Jessie said no, that it was Mrs. Wiley's horse, and then the two got into a conversation about horses and shows, and Dara asked Jessie if she showed, and Jessie said yes, sometimes. . . .

And Kate slipped outside, dragging her feet through the dirt, feeling truly miserable.

She walked to the fence around the paddock and pulled herself up to sit there, her chin in her hands. She had been sitting there, feeling very sorry for herself, for maybe fifteen minutes, when Dara appeared, leading the dazzling Arpeggio out of the barn. Behind her Jessie led Jonathan, and the two girls were talking as if they'd been friends for years.

Before they could see her, Kate jumped from the fence and headed back into the barn. From the window in the tack room she watched the girls take the horses into the outside ring. Dara held Arpeggio back, called something to Jessie, and Jessie started taking Jonathan through the dressage exercises.

Then Dara mounted, and Jessie watched as Arpeggio executed every singe exercise with a perfection that made Kate want to cry. *This is ridiculous!* Kate told herself firmly. I'm not going to stand here and make myself sick with envy, she thought. It would be best, she decided, if she went into the house and started dinner. She could finish the barn chores later when Jessie and Dara were gone.

But Kate couldn't help watching from the kitchen window when the Mercedes pulled in. She watched Dara introducing Jessie to Mrs. Cooper, and she watched while they shoved Jessie's bike into the trunk and all took off together.

The next day at school Kate decided to act as if nothing happened. She met Jessie at their lockers, and at lunch they talked about the upcoming show. Not once did Jessie mention her ride with Dara yesterday. And, Kate couldn't help but notice, Dara wasn't sitting at their table today. Pete and Bruce kept stealing looks across the lunchroom, to the table where she was sitting with Doug Lyons and some other juniors.

"And I hope she stays there," Monica said, following the boys' glances.

"She's not so bad, Monica," Jessie said.

Kate excused herself, before she said something she would wish she hadn't, and went to the library to read her book.

She didn't see Jessie until later that afternoon, at the stables. Kate was already out on Night Owl, letting him have his run before she got down to drilling him in the ring. She heard hooves pounding behind her and turned to see Jessie, astride Jonathan, galloping toward her.

Kate reined Night Owl in and waited, then the girls rode along in silence for several minutes.

The horses hacked along on a loose rein, heads lowered, necks extended, the picture of relaxed enjoyment.

Finally, Jessie said, "Maybe I should have asked Dara to come on the trails with us."

"No," Kate snapped, and then, catching herself, said, "I'd just rather not ride with someone I don't know."

"Have you seen her ride?"

"Not really," Kate said, unwilling to admit she had spied on them.

Jessie went on, "She's pretty good. But boy, is her mother a pain. They gave me a ride home, and she was nagging at Dara the whole time. Then Dara got mad at her, and Mrs. Cooper said she was only trying to help and that 'you should watch your mouth, young lady.' It seems Mrs. Cooper is upset because she wanted Mr. Yon to be Dara's trainer, but he said no."

"He's moving to Florida," Kate said. "I had a little talk with Mrs. Cooper, too, and I didn't like her, either."

"Well, I guess it's no wonder Dara is the way she is."

How is she? Kate was tempted to ask.

"So anyway," Jessie said, "I got pretty tired of Mrs. Cooper telling me how good Dara was, so I told her you were pretty good, too."

Kate turned in her saddle to glare at Jessie. "Will you please stop doing that?"

"Why? You *are* as good as Dara is. And I wish

you'd take Night Owl into the ring and school with her."

"Do me a favor," Kate said, "just don't talk about the Coopers, all right?"

"What are you mad at now?"

"I'm not mad. Yes, I *am* mad. It was bad enough when you invited half the school to watch me show, but now with Dara there, I'll really look like a fool. And yesterday, on the worst day of my life, you go out riding with Dara."

Jessie gaped at her. "But you'd already ridden! And she asked me to ride with her."

Staring grimly ahead, Kate put her leg to Night Owl, rose forward in the saddle, and leaned over his neck, giving him his head. The big horse responded instantly and took off at a run up the hill. The wind rushed by Kate's face. Behind her she could hear the sound of Jonathan thundering along.

They crested the top of the hill. Below them the trail dipped gently and then flattened out to run alongside a stream. Kate let Night Owl go. He ran, his mane flying and stinging her face where she leaned close to his neck.

She let him run along the streambed, and when the trail narrowed and crossed over the shallow water, she eased him to a stop.

Jessie came up alongside them, her face flushed. Jonathan was breathing hard; there was lather on his neck. Night Owl stood quietly as if he hadn't moved at all.

"I can't stand it when we're not friends," Jessie said softly.

Kate looked over at her remorsefully. "We're still friends, Jessie. I'm being a jerk. I'm sorry. But everything's going wrong. Now Mom is going in the hospital to have her knee operated on for sure."

"Why didn't you tell me?"

"Because I was being a jerk."

"When does she have to go?"

"Tonight. And she'll be in the hospital for almost a week. Jessie, will you stay with me until Dad gets back from the hospital? I need help with the chores, but I also need some company."

"Of course I will," Jessie said. "That's what friends are for."

Chapter 10

JESSIE sat cross-legged on one of the beds in Kate's room. A slow, steady drizzle pattered on the leaves of the maple just outside the bedroom window.

"It's so peaceful here," Jessie said. "I love this old house."

Kate was playing with the ends of her hair, rocking back and forth on her bed. She said, "I'm scared."

"Your mom?" Jessie asked softly.

"No," Kate said quickly, knowing Jessie was thinking of how she'd felt when her own mother was sick." I know she's going to be okay. It's my riding, Jess. I'm terrible."

"Your riding?" Jessie said in surprise. "Kate Wiley is scared because of her riding?" She looked around, then back at Kate. "This *is* Kate Wiley I'm talking to, isn't it? The rider who three times in a row last year scored higher at eventing meets than anybody else? You *are* that Kate Wiley, right?"

"No," Kate said, her eyes heavy with misery. "I'm not. I don't know what happened to her."

"Is something really wrong?" Jessie asked, her voice now filled with concern. "I know you keep telling me that Night Owl's not doing well, but you have a tendency to exaggerate the bad parts of your riding and not see the good parts."

"Sometimes I do," Kate admitted. "It makes me nervous to have people tell me how good I am. It makes me feel like I have too much to live up to. But this time I'm not exaggerating. If you'd ridden with me yesterday, you'd know how bad things really are." There was a bite to Kate's words.

Jessie ignored the comment and said, "Kate, it won't be the end of the world if you don't take a ribbon on Saturday."

"Want to bet?" Kate sighed and looked at her friend. "Mr. Yon is sending some of his students to The Hill to see me ride. He thinks that when they see what a good job Mom has done with me and Night Owl, they'll want to come here with their horses when he closes up."

"Oh-oh," Jessie said.

"Yeah. Oh-oh. Windcroft might just as well kiss those people good-bye once they get a look at me and Night Owl. Especially with Dara there doing everything right and Mrs. Cooper talking about how you can't get a good trainer in Connecticut. She thinks Windcroft is one step above the pits. And if I back out, that won't look very good either. And everyone at school will think I did it because of Dara."

"I wish you weren't so down on Dara," Jessie said.

"And I wish you'd stop trying to make her into my friend."

Jessie sighed, then said, "Night Owl can't be as bad as you think he is."

Kate stared down at her hands, her eyes miserable. "You know, last year, how those people at Spruce Ridge were telling Mom that we ought to be looking for a new horse, because Night Owl wasn't good enough to take me where I wanted to go? What if they were right? What if Night Owl can't compete above the novice level?"

"Stop!" Jessie said heatedly. "I refuse to believe that Night Owl can't do training level. Now, I don't know how much help I'll be," she said, "but I'm willing to watch the two of you and see if I can come up with something. Do you want me to come home with you early? Or will you wait to ride until I get to the barn?"

"I can't ask you to miss class," Kate said, a note of hope creeping into her voice. "That would be really selfish. But, could you stay a little late tomorrow night? Maybe we can get a few minutes in after Dara schools."

"Won't that look weird? Both of us standing around while it gets dark, waiting for her to get out of the ring so you can ride?"

"I don't care how it looks," Kate said, her temper rising again. "That's the only way I'll do it."

"Okay," Jessie said, "Calm down. We'll do it your way. I'll work with you tomorrow and I'll bet you a pizza you've exaggerated things way out of proportion."

"Make it a big one," Kate said glumly, "and don't forget the pepperoni."

The next afternoon Kate busied herself in the barn while she waited for Dara to finish up in the ring. Twice she'd gone to the window to watch. Dara and Arpeggio were going as smoothly as if they'd just been oiled. She leaned on the broom now and stared at Night Owl. He stared back at her with troubled eyes.

"Don't give me that what-in-the-world-is-wrong look," she said, "because I don't have a clue. I was hoping you could explain the problems we're having."

He blew at her softly. She reached her hand into his stall and scratched his ears. "I still love you," she said, "even though you've turned dim-witted."

"Kate? Oh there you are," Jessie said, coming down the aisle toward her. "How's your mom?"

Kate had taken the day off from school to visit Anne in the hospital.

"Lots better. The doctor says she can come home on Monday."

"That's great news," Jessie said, and smiled.

"Yeah," Kate agreed. "At least she'll still be in the hospital on Sunday when the scores from my dressage test come in, so they can sedate her."

Jessie laughed. "Pete was asking about you. He said he was going to call to see if you were sick."

"That's nice," Kate said. A week ago that would have made her happy, but right now she was too upset to care.

"And," Jessie went on, "here's the big news. Monica and Bruce are going to the movies this weekend."

"Hurray," Kate said without enthusiasm.

"It's getting to be harder and harder to cheer you up," Jessie said, with her hands on her hips.

"Then don't try," Kate replied. She glanced out the window. Dara was dismounting Arpeggio. "I'll get Night Owl tacked up." She finished with the brushes and put on Night Owl's saddle and bridle, and checked the window again. Dara was walking Arpeggio slowly toward the barn. "Let's go," Kate said grimly, plunking her riding helmet on.

Outside, Kate took a shortcut across the grass so she wouldn't have to pass close to Dara and talk to her; she waited at the ring for Jessie to open the gate for her. Jessie climbed up to sit on the top rail while Kate trotted the Owl around the ring several times to warm him up. "Are you ready?" Jessie called out finally. When Kate nodded yes, she asked, "What are you having the most trouble with?"

"Everything."

"Circle him in a working trot," Jessie said, "then try a half-halt into a canter."

Kate circled Night Owl in the upper half of the field. When she had gone around once, she asked for the half-halt and then for the canter. Night Owl broke from a trot to a walk, then lumbered into a heavy canter.

Kate reined him in sharply. "Let's try it again," she said grimly, and did the exercise a second time with no better results.

"Maybe you're pulling back too sharply for the half-halt," Jessie said uncertainly, "or not giving him the signal to canter soon enough."

Kate circled him once again, and this time Night Owl stopped completely before picking up the canter. Kate felt a rush of anger and for the first time in all the years since she'd had Night Owl, she was furious at him.

Jessie eyed her nervously. "Okay, forget the half-halt for now. Track right at a working trot, then come down the diagonal at an extended trot."

Kate set her jaw and brought Night Owl alongside the rail, trotting him halfway around the ring. She could feel him turn sharply and awkwardly in the corner. When she headed him across the ring on a diagonal, asking for a longer stride, he broke from a trot into a canter.

She stopped him and sat in the saddle, trying to get herself under control.

Jessie hopped off the fence and ran up to her. "I'm not sure, but maybe if . . ."

"*Maybe if* isn't good enough," Kate said, glaring at the barn, sure Dara was in there watching her. She ran a hand down Night Owl's neck. "What's happened to us?" Kate asked Jessie in despair.

Jessie shook her head. "Maybe he's just bored," she offered.

Kate looked at her friend. "That's possible," she admitted. "He does hate ring work."

"Maybe when you get him to the show, he'll be fine. You know what a ham he is when he has an audience." Jessie was warming to her own idea.

"That's true," Kate said, a little glimmer of hope lighting her eyes. "Oh Jessie, wouldn't it be wonderful if that's all it is?"

"I'll just bet when you get to The Hill, Night Owl will be his old self again," Jessie said with an assurance she didn't quite feel, and sneaked her hands behind her back to cross her fingers.

Chapter 11

AT 5:00 A.M. on the morning of the show, the alarm in Kate's room jangled noisily. Kate reached out disjointedly in the dark to turn it off, knocking it to the floor with a loud bang.

"Wouldn't it have been nicer just to call me softly?" Jessie asked sleepily from the other bed. Kate hung almost upside down, scrambling under her bed for the clock, its alarm still ringing. She located it finally and clicked it firmly silent. "I think it's safe to say you've wakened everyone between here and Hartford," Jessie said.

Kate tossed her bedclothes back and stood up, shivering. "I'll take my shower first. That'll give you five more minutes in bed."

"Thank you," Jessie said gratefully.

In five minutes Kate was back, buttoning the front of her riding shirt. "Your turn," she said.

While Jessie stumbled toward the bathroom, Kate pulled her hair carefully into a tight, smooth braid, then pinned it to the back of her head. At her mirror she applied a few light dabs of makeup, something she hardly ever bothered with, but when she was showing, she wanted to look her absolute best.

She climbed into her beige jodhpurs, which clung to her slim hips like a second skin. Her navy blue riding jacket hung on a hanger behind the door. Kate wouldn't put that on until the last minute, just before she was due in the ring.

Knocking on the bathroom door, she called, "I'll go down and start breakfast," then hurried through the dark hallway, stopping to knock on her father's door. When he mumbled a groggy answer, she went on down to the kitchen.

At the foot of the stairs she stopped. Her chest suddenly felt as if it were locked in a vise. Take a deep breath, Kate said to herself. Everything's going to be all right. Jessie solved the problem. Night Owl just needs an audience.

Within fifteen minutes her father and Jessie were in the kitchen. "I made hot cocoa," Kate said, handing her dad a mug.

He cupped his hands around it and sipped it slowly. "I'll bet the horses are hungry. You two go out in the barn and get them fed and watered. I'll make breakfast."

Outside, the sky was a pearly gray with just a thin line of gold along the horizon. Kate and

Jessie hurried along the path, hugging themselves. Kate pushed the barn door open and flicked on the lights.

"Please don't let him have rubbed his braids out," Kate prayed, going directly to Night Owl's stall. "Let one thing have gone right."

The horse was standing sideways, his head turned toward the door, the taut arch of his neck outlined in tiny little loops of braided mane that Kate had spent hours on the previous evening. She looked them over closely. Not one of them had loosened during the night. "Thank you," she told him. He surveyed her with troubled eyes, which she avoided meeting.

While the horses were eating, Kate and Jessie stood in the doorway of the barn and watched the sun come up. "This is almost the best part of showing," Jessie said. "I love being up and in the barn this early." Kate looked at her sideways. "Well I don't like *getting* up," Jessie said, "but once I'm up, I like it."

"Here comes Dara," Jessie said abruptly, spotting two headlights shining in the drive.

Kate turned her head as Dara got out of the car and came toward them. "Is she limping?" Kate asked sarcastically.

Jessie poked her in the ribs.

"We fed Arpeggio for you," Jessie said as Dara entered the barn.

"You did?" Dara said in her husky voice. "Thanks. It's going to be a perfect day." She looked up at the sky, now turning a brilliant, rosy gold. "Not a cloud anywhere."

For some of us, Kate thought. Mr. Wiley stepped out on the back steps and rang an old-fashioned dinner bell. "My dad's making breakfast," Kate said. "Want some?" It was not a gracious invitation, but it was the best Kate could do.

Dara looked at her a long moment before saying, "No thanks, I ate before I left the house. Besides, I have to braid Arpeggio."

"Now?" Jessie asked. "We're leaving in an hour."

"I can do it in an hour," Dara said.

"Then you must have some secret method," Jessie said. "It takes Kate and me half a day."

Dara smiled. "I do."

"Naturally. Something you learned at Concordia, no doubt," Kate said.

"Yes." Dara turned cool eyes on her. "If you like"—she directed the words to Jessie—"I'll show you."

Kate moved off toward the house as Dara and Jessie continued to talk.

A few moments later Jessie caught up with Kate on the way back to the house. "Why are you so touchy around her?" she asked.

"Because," Kate said.

"That's no reason."

"It is for me. Could we just forget Dara, please. I have enough on my mind today. This could just probably end up being the worst day of my life."

"Mine, too," Jessie said.

"You're not even showing," Kate said, stamping up the back stairs and holding the door open.

"I never thought I'd ever be grateful not to show, but believe me I am. You have enough nerves for both of us."

They both went inside to a big breakfast of ham and eggs, and the subject of Dara was dropped. For a while.

"Well," Mr. Wiley said when they were finished eating, "time to get going. I'll back the van down to the barn. You girls collect your stuff and meet me there."

"I used to hate this part," Jessie said as they walked toward the driveway. "Time-Out was always a real headache to load."

"The Owl thinks the van is his second home. Unless he's forgotten that, too."

The big green van with WINDCROFT STABLES painted on it in neat white letters was waiting for them. Dara had already lugged the hay nets in and tied one in each stall in the van to keep the horses happy on the ride to The Hill, and was standing talking to Kate's father. "We had our own trailer in Pennsylvania," Kate heard her say. "It was too much of a hassle trying to get room on the stable's van."

"How many horses did they take to shows?" Jessie asked Kate softly.

"Hundreds," Kate said. "Thousands."

"Ready?" Mr. Wiley asked.

"Ready," Kate said, and went in to get the Owl.

He was so achingly beautiful, all shiny and clean, with his mane braided and his tail brushed. Too bad his head had developed a hole someplace that leaked out everything she'd ever taught him.

He loaded with no trouble at all, and so did Arpeggio, and in a matter of minutes they were ready to leave.

"Are we all going in the van?" Mr. Wiley asked.

"My mom will be back in a second," Dara said. "I'll be going with her."

Kate opened the door and climbed up into the van. "Then we'll see you there."

"See you there," Jessie echoed, and climbed up next to Kate. "I don't care what you think," Jessie said. "I feel sorry for her with a mother like that."

"Don't," Kate said. "Dara's got every single thing going her way. If you want to feel sorry for someone, feel sorry for me. I'm about to make a fool of myself and ruin my mother's whole career."

At The Hill the van pulled into the open parking fields. "Look at all the people," Kate said. The grounds were like a medieval fair. Tents had been set up for the judges and officials. Horses of all colors and sizes milled around, and riders in jackets and breeches stood talking in little clumps. Sometimes, at the bigger shows, the competition went on for three days. The dressage class would be held the first day, the stadium jumping class the next, and the outdoor course would be run on the third day. But as this wasn't one of the big shows, all three events would be run in one day.

Kate saw that the jump ring was full of riders getting in some last-minute practice. It looked like sure suicide, horses and riders coming every which way, shouting "Heads up," and hoping they were heard. Soon, she'd have to get Night Owl in there for his pre-show workout.

"I *am* sorry I'm not showing," Jessie said, looking out at all the hubbub.

"I'll give you my spot," Kate offered. "Well, let's get out and unload Night Owl, walk the kinks out, and show him the crowd. See if all the excitement has brought his memory back."

As they approached the van, Kate stopped dead. "Who's that?" she asked. Someone was helping her father slide the heavy loading ramp into place. "Tell me it's a total stranger."

"It's a total stranger," Jessie said.

"It is not!" Kate cried in a strangled voice. "It's Pete Hastings."

When the ramp was in place, Dara appeared from behind the van, Mrs. Cooper close beside her. "Which one is yours?" Pete asked, squinting into the dark van.

"The gray," Dara said, walking lightly up the ramp to untie Arpeggio and bring him down. He came prancing down the ramp as if he owned the world and everything in it.

Kate wished she could hate him, but she couldn't

hate a horse. "He's gorgeous, isn't he?" she said. "And look, Pete thinks so, too."

"Kate," Jessie said, "are we going to stand here all day?"

"Now, that's a good idea," Kate said. "That's the first good idea you've had since you said, 'Come to the show, you guys, and let Kate show you what she does.'" She felt like hiding.

But it was too late, Pete had seen them. "Hi." He smiled in a way that made her heart race, even as nervous as she was. "You look great," he said, looking her over approvingly.

"Thanks." Kate felt herself blushing. "Have you ever been to a show?" She knew it was a dumb question, but she couldn't think of anything else to say.

Pete grinned and brushed a shock of sandy hair out of his eyes. "I don't think I even knew horse shows existed before." He hesitated and his eyes grew serious. "Before you, that is."

Kate's heart skipped a beat. Somehow those words—and the way Pete was looking at her— were changing her whole mood.

"Hey," Jessie called from the van. "Let's get Night Owl down. He's probably lonely up there without his buddy."

"They're friends?" Pete asked. "I never thought of horses needing friends."

"Everybody needs friends," Dara said. "I'm going to try to get into the ring to school. It looks like it's emptied out a little."

Kate looked over at the ring. The first rush of

riders had left and now only three horses were making their way quietly around the ring. "I'd better get in there, too," she said. "Jessie, will you help me tack up?"

"Can I do anything?" Pete asked.

Kate stood at the top of the ramp and looked down at him, then grinned. "You already did," she told him.

Chapter 12

By the time Kate got to the jumping ring, the only horse in it was Arpeggio. Dara, in her usual graceful way, took him calmly over each jump in both directions. Mrs. Cooper stood by the rail, calling out corrections. Some of them were downright wrong, and Kate looked quickly to see if Dara was listening. She may have been listening, but she wasn't obeying.

Kate walked Night Owl from jump to jump, letting him look his fill. Then she circled him at a slow trot, posting him to a canter before putting him over the lowest of the jumps. He went easily, and Kate's spirits lifted a little. Maybe all he did need was the excitement of a show.

She tried Night Owl over the brush jump next, and the oxer. He was going well. Then they tried the in and out. He missed the timing of the second part of the jump and just barely scrambled over it. Any encouragement Kate may have felt at his earlier performance drained right out the bottom of her boots.

"It looks like two strides, but it rides better in one big one," Dara called from behind her. "See if you can get him to extend a little coming into the first one." Kate stared at Dara. It was the kind of thing her mother would have said if she'd been here.

"Thanks," Kate said, and tried it again, this time pushing Night Owl a little harder. He covered the distance between the two jumps in one stride and jumped the second part of the in and out in a huge arc-shaped leap that took Kate's breath away. Well, it wasn't graceful, but at least he got over it. She circled him once more, setting him toward the brush jump. Three strides before it, he stopped dead, and Kate almost lost her balance.

"What time is your dressage test, dear?" Mrs. Cooper's voice floated over the ring.

Kate, her head reeling from the fact that Night Owl had just refused a jump, looked at Mrs. Cooper. "Mine?" she asked.

"Yes, dear. I want to be sure I see it."

Kate reluctantly told her the time. "Oh, that's lucky. Dara is right after you. We'll all be there watching and cheering you on."

Isn't that lucky, Kate thought, and turned Night Owl toward the jump again, this time applying a light tap of her riding crop to get him over it.

"Mother, why don't you see if you can get me

something to drink," Dara called. "My throat's dry as a bone."

"Well, I did want to see you school," Mrs. Cooper said uncertainly.

"Please?" Dara asked. Mrs. Cooper stood on tiptoe to sight the refreshment stand and, after asking Kate if she wanted anything, walked away.

Her place outside the ring was taken almost immediately by Pete, Monica, and Bruce.

"Kate," Monica called. "You look fabulous!"

Dara heard her and laughed good-naturedly. "One thing about Monica," Dara said. "You always know what's important to her."

"Can you get him to go over those fencey-looking things?" Monica asked.

"I can," Kate said, "but he's already been over them twice. You'll have to wait for my class this afternoon."

"This afternoon? Are we staying that *long*?" There was a hurried consultation between Monica and Bruce. "Don't you do anything in the morning?"

"The dressage tests are in the morning," Mrs. Cooper said, coming back with a soda for Dara. "Are you friends of the girls? How nice of you to come. You'll find the dressage class wonderful. We'll go together and I'll explain the tests to you."

Well, that was the final straw. Any hope Kate had that her friends wouldn't know how badly she had done was gone. She was sure Mrs. Cooper would point out every mistake she made.

The ring was filling up again. "Here comes the mob," Dara said. "Time to leave." Kate followed her out.

Monica and Bruce headed for the refreshment stand, but Pete walked easily alongside Kate, asking her questions about the show. Kate tried to answer him, but her mind was filled with visions of the coming disaster.

At the van Jessie was waiting. "How did we do?" Kate shook her head. "Where's Dara?" Jessie asked.

"I don't know. Her mother carted her off someplace. Where's my dad?"

"He's over by the dressage arena with ..." Jessie stopped suddenly and pretended to be busy with something.

"With who?" Kate asked tensely. "It's the people Mr. Yon sent down, isn't it?"

"Maybe they're just some people he knows that I don't know," Jessie said.

"Yeah," Kate said, "and maybe that's the moon, not the sun."

"Is something wrong?" Pete asked.

Kate saw that Night Owl was nuzzling him, but this time even Pete couldn't make her feel better. "If I knew where to begin, I'd tell you," she said, and sighed. Then she turned to Jessie. "How many people were there?"

"Where?" Jessie asked, looking around innocently.

"With my dad."

"Oh, Kate, I don't know. Maybe four or five."

"I'm going to withdraw. Don't look at me that way."

"I can't believe you're saying this."

Kate buried her face in her hands. "Jessie, you know how bad he is. Even just now in the jump ring. And jumping's the thing he does best. Is that what I'm going to show Mr. Yon's students? Something's happened. My riding is awful, and the worst thing of all is I don't know why."

"I do," Dara said quietly from behind Kate.

Kate swung around.

Dara looked at her with a sympathetic grin. "I didn't mean to eavesdrop, but I couldn't help hearing. Look, I know you're not crazy about me, but I really think I can tell you what's wrong."

"Something your trainer in Pennsylvania told you, I'll bet," Kate said.

"Actually, it is," Dara said in her lazy way. "I'd probably dislike him as much as you do if I had to stand around and listen to your mother tell me how great he was. But the truth is, he really was wonderful. And he told me something that I think will help you."

"Is it a magic spell?" Kate asked. "Because that's what it's going to take to get Night Owl retrained before my dressage test."

Dara shook her head. "He doesn't need retraining. He's been trained beautifully. He's doing every single thing you ask of him. The trouble is, you're asking him to do stuff without knowing it. Your problem is body language. Look," Dara said, when Kate continued to stare at her, "bring Night

Owl over there." She gestured toward an open expanse of field. "I'll show you what I mean."

"Do it, Kate," Jessie urged.

Without a word Kate mounted Night Owl and walked him over to the empty part of the parking field.

"Now, try this," Dara said. "Let your head and arms hang loose, just let everything relax and take three deep breaths. Think about all the tension draining out of your body, really think about it. Now, just like that, without straightening up, put the Owl to a walk on a loose rein. Then after a couple minutes, sit up and tighten the muscles in your stomach, the way you do when you get nervous, and see what happens."

Kate touched her legs to Night Owl and he obediently walked out. After four or five strides she sat up and drew her stomach muscles into a tight knot. Night Owl stopped dead. Kate looked at Dara in surprise. "But I didn't ask him to stop."

"Yes, you did. He's so attuned to your signals that when you tightened up, he felt it. You tightened everything up, your arms, your legs, you sat deeper into the saddle. Night Owl felt every one of the changes and decided you were asking him to stop. So he did."

Kate stared at Dara under drawn brows, then took the relaxed position again, urged Night Owl forward, sat up again, and tightened her muscles. And again the big horse stopped. "That's amazing," she said.

"Now, try this," Dara said. She gave Kate a few

more relaxing exercises to try, and with each one the effect on Night Owl was astounding.

Kate sighed. "I wish I'd found this out before when I could have worked on it." Dara looked at her steadily and Kate dropped her eyes. Of course, if she'd given Dara half a chance before this, Dara would have told her.

"You've got an hour before your test," Dara said.

"Dara," Kate began, but she couldn't find the right words.

Dara smiled her slow smile. "Don't withdraw," she said. "I've been looking forward to riding against you since Mr. Yon told my mother how great you were."

"He told your mother that?" Kate said.

"Why do you think my mother's made such a point of telling you how good I am? It's all still there," Dara added. "All your skill. Your thinking just got a little short-circuited."

"Dara, Dara, for heaven's sake, where are you?" Mrs. Cooper's voice trilled. "There's someone here I want you to meet."

"Probably some poor unsuspecting riding coach," Dara said, and grinned, "about to get the thrill of a lifetime. See you in the ring?"

Kate waved as she left. Jessie ran over to Kate. "What did she tell you?"

"Jessie, I'm gong to put Night Owl through his paces. Now you tell me honestly, *honestly,* if you see a difference."

She circled Night Owl, first at an easy trot, then

with a half-halt into a canter. The change from one gait to another was smooth as silk. She rode him halfway around the circle and put him on a course that would cut the imaginary ring in half. The turn was a smooth arc. At the end of the diagonal run she turned him again and asked him for a canter. Instead he slowed to a walk. She stopped him and took two deep breaths, then let her arms and head hang loosely for a minute and tried again. This time he slipped into the canter on the tight lead beautifully.

"Kate," Jessie said, her voice shaky as if she were afraid to break some kind of spell, "what's happened to him? He's perfect."

"It was me," Kate said. "I was the problem." She explained quickly to Jessie what Dara had told her. "Watch again." She went through some more exercises. Each time the results were the same. When Night Owl misread a cue, Kate made herself relax and the horse responded with perfection.

She reined Night Owl in and sat looking at Jessie. "Now all I have to worry about is everyone from school. And Pete."

"Well, don't. You could fall flat on your face and Pete would still think you're wonderful. And Monica has already told me that she *loooooves* the way your breeches look with that 'trim, little riding jacket—very slimming.' She's planning on taking up riding just so she can wear jodhpurs and a riding jacket."

Kate laughed nervously. "How much time do I have?"

Jessie checked her watch. "Thirty-five minutes. Remember, all you have to do is think relaxing thoughts—waterfalls, raindrops, the ocean—"

"Shoulder-ins, half-halts, half-passes."

"Kate!" Jessie said with exasperation.

"I'm only kidding," Kate said, and grinned. "I just have to stay loose and try not to give Night Owl the wrong signals." Beneath her the bay snorted his approval, and she leaned down to pat his neck. "And you," she said, "will be absolutely perfect!"

Chapter 13

KATE brought Night Owl as far as the holding area next to the dressage ring and let him walk quietly on a loose rein. The little silver bell that the judge used to summon each competitor rang out musically. "Number sixty-seven, please," the starter called. A light sorrel horse paused at the entrance. Kate turned her back. She didn't want to watch. Inside her head she was singing every song she could think of.

"Katie May!"

She turned to see her father standing just outside the holding area. He held up his hand; his fingers were crossed.

She grinned her thanks, and he made his way back toward the arena.

She could hear the sorrel's footfalls inside the arena, but louder than that was the thump of her heart. "I think I can, I think I can," the words from a story that her mother read to her when she was a little girl came suddenly into her head. She kept repeating them to herself. "I really think I can," she sang softly. "I know I can, I know I can, I really know I can."

The silver bell tinkled again, and just for a moment Kate felt her stomach knot painfully. But she forced the muscles to relax.

"Number sixty-eight, please," the starter called.

"Ready," Kate said, sitting up straight in the saddle. She felt under the lapel of her riding jacket for the little gold horseshoe her dad had given her just before her first show. "As we'll ever be," she added under her breath.

She had sixty seconds to get into the arena, and she used every one of them. She brought Night Owl alongside the outside fence of the arena and trotted him the entire length of it. His movements were strong and full of energy, and when she got to the short side, near the entrance, she asked him for a small circle, then turned him between the two tubs of evergreen that marked the in-gate. Finally, she trotted him in a straight, steady line down the center of the arena.

In front of the judges she halted him. Night Owl stopped dead still, his head up, looking straight ahead. Kate passed both reins into her left hand, dropped her right arm straight down at her side, and saluted the judges by nodding her head. When the judges had acknowledged her, she picked up the reins with both hands and began the test. She drove every thought out of her mind except the love she felt for Night Owl, and the joy she felt in riding. The figures of the test presented themselves to her as if they were written on some kind of cue sheet in her brain.

Proceed, working trot, sitting, the prompter in her brain said, *then track to the right. A little fast, slow him down.*

The turn in the first corner was only a bit awkward, but Night Owl was always stiff in the turns. This time, if anything, he was a little more relaxed than usual.

Working canter, right lead. Kate signaled him that the change was coming. He hesitated, then slipped into the new gait.

Another twenty-meter circle in the center of the ring. Keep it round, keep it round, Kate told herself. Now, down to a trot, Big Bird. As if she were whispering in his ear, he did as she'd asked.

At the short end of the arena, almost directly in front of the judges, she asked for a working walk. It was too slow, she could feel it, but decided not to ask for more, afraid he might go back again to his trot.

In the corner she turned him and set him on a diagonal to the opposite corner of the ring, giving him a long rein. His neck relaxed and stretched out. She applied the slightest pressure with her calves and gently fingered the reins. Night Owl responded and picked up the pace as Kate looked steadily at the corner they were approaching to keep him on a straight line.

As they reached the corner, she turned him and they headed back on the same diagonal. When they reached the halfway mark on the short side of the arena, she asked the horse to halt. He did, perfectly, without any extra movement. This was almost the worst part of the whole test. Night Owl had to stand absolutely still for five seconds, without even twitching a muscle.

Kate counted mentally—one one thousand, two one thousand—never had mere seconds passed so slowly—until she reached five. Then, releasing her control over him, she allowed Night Owl to go forward into a working trot.

There were more circles and more canters, a change of leads, and a change of reins. But after that perfect, heart-stopping halt, the rest of the test passed in a blur.

Soon they were trotting down the center line again, straight for the judges. Kate brought Night Owl to a smooth, quiet halt and saluted the judges.

At the judges' signal, she urged Night Owl into a walk and turned back toward the entrance, moving close to the edge of the long side of the arena. He was walking in a jaunty, I-did-pretty-good stride, and Kate felt like a newly crowned Miss America must feel.

As she left the arena, she could see her father at the gate and Jessie beside him.

"That was super; that was wonderful," Jessie cried, running up to her, "that was the best test I've ever seen you ride."

"Is it bad manners to kiss a horse?" Mr. Wiley

asked, planting a big smack on Night Owl's neck.
Night Owl tossed his head and danced sideways.

Kate was laughing—with relief and pure joy.
"Hold it," she said. "Let me dismount before we
trample somebody." She slipped from the saddle
and, grasping Night Owl firmly by the bridle, led
him to the far side of the holding area.

Pete Hastings, hands thrust into his back pockets, picked his way through the crowd toward
them. "You were incredible!" he said. "Mrs. Cooper was explaining all those moves—"

"You mean she started to," Monica cut in, "but
about halfway though, she just stopped talking."

"I'll *bet* she did," Jessie said, rocking from her
heels to her toes, her arms clasped behind her
back.

"Well, it definitely looks like fun," Monica announced. "And I'm definitely going to try it. I can't
wait to wear one of those sleek little jackets."

The silvery tinkle of the judges' bell rang out
again. "Hey guys," Kate said, "that's Dara. Dad,
would you take Night Owl back to the van for me
and untack him? I'd like to watch."

"Sure," her father said. "Come on, big guy, you
deserve a good massage. Got to keep you in
shape for the jumping class and the outside
course." Kate wasn't worried about those. The
worst part was over.

Kate turned to the ring where Dara's first test
had already begun. Arpeggio was stunning, and
Dara looked her beautiful best. Kate concentrated
and tried to be objective. Arpeggio was better in

the corners than Night Owl, but what else was new? His walk was livelier, but Kate thought his canter was a little too fast. At the long, nerve-racking halt, he seemed to shift his weight as if he were about to step forward. Kate heard Mrs. Cooper sigh in exasperation.

Dara's test was good, very good, Kate thought. Better than hers? She really couldn't tell. They'd have to wait for the judges' score, and even then it wasn't finished. But she knew that Night Owl would give Arpeggio a run for his money over the jumps and on the outside course.

When Dara left the arena, Kate hurried over to her. "You were great," she said.

"Thanks," Dara said, blushing a little. "So were you."

"You watched? Before your own test?" That was something Kate couldn't ever do.

"I couldn't help myself," Dara said. "I had to see if you were as good as Mr. Yon said you were."

"And?" Kate asked, half afraid of the answer.

"You are."

"Well, you can take some of the credit for that."

"I just pointed the way, you and Night Owl did the rest."

"Dara," Kate began, and paused.

"Are you going to tell me how grateful you are, and how you misjudged me, and how you'd like for us to be friends?" Dara said in her slightly off-center way.

"Something like that," Kate said, blushing furiously.

"Good. Then we've got that over with. We're going to have the best time," Dara said with a quick, wicked grin, "trying to outdo each other."

"Well"—Mrs. Cooper huffed up to them—"I hope you're satisfied. I told you to let me find you a trainer, but, no, you wanted to wait and work with Mrs. Wiley." She turned to Kate. "That's not to say your mother isn't a good coach, but Dara is used to professionals." She snapped her head back toward her daughter. "We'll have it your way; you always were stubborn. But just remember, the rules haven't changed." And with that, she marched off and disappeared in the stands.

Dara slipped off Arpeggio and the girls started leading the tall thoroughbred. "What rules?" Kate asked.

"Oh, when we bought Arpeggio, my mother told me that he was mine as long as I came in first in most of my classes."

"And if you don't?" Kate said.

"I lose him."

Kate looked at Dara in astonishment.

"I know, it makes her sound like a real witch, but except for this horse stuff, she's really okay. I've learned to live with all her rules and regulations. And besides, she thinks she's motivating me."

"*Motivating* you? By threatening to take away your horse?"

"Well, it's kind of complicated. See, she always

wanted to ride, and never could, her family was just too poor. But my dad isn't poor, and we can afford a horse for me, so she's determined that I'm going to do what she never could, which means competing at the top."

Kate mulled all that over as they walked, then said slowly, "Knowing how your mother was going to react, you still helped me ride the best dressage test I've ever ridden."

Dara cocked her head and gave Kate a lopsided smile. "It wouldn't have been any fun beating you if you weren't at your best."

"What makes you think you beat me?"

"Because I'm good," Dara said, and grinned.

Kate felt a rush of hot pride and opened her mouth to retort, but Jessie elbowed her.

"Hey," Jessie said, linking one arm through Kate's and one through Dara's, "the fact is, you're *both* very good."

Later, while they tended their horses, Kate did some mental arithmetic, trying to figure out her score and Dara's. It was no use. She'd have to wait for the judge's voice to come over the PA system with the scores—the *real* scores.

Chapter 14

THE dressage tests had been over for almost an hour, but the scores still hadn't been posted. Kate and Dara were listening for the announcement and leading Night Owl and Arpeggio around the bare area of the parking lot.

Kate's father was off somewhere with Pietro Yon's clients. At least, she thought, Dad's keeping them out of my sight. It still made her nervous, knowing she was being judged by them, too. Her and the whole farm!

The other kids had gone to get something to eat, and now Kate saw them all coming back. Pete and Jessie were carrying sandwiches for Kate and Dara, and Monica and Bruce were talking a mile a minute.

From the other direction Mrs. Cooper came bearing down on them, her small face screwed up in a frown.

124

They all converged near Dara and Kate and the horses at the same moment that the outdoor PA system crackled to life and a hollow-sounding voice echoed across to them.

Kate couldn't catch all the opening words; she heard only "unforeseeable complications and unexpected delays," but she did catch the rest: "The Hill officials apologize for the inconvenience. Dressage scores will not be posted until later in the afternoon."

"Well," Mrs. Cooper said, breathless with outrage, "this certainly isn't Pennsylvania!"

The dressage scores still weren't posted when Kate took Night Owl in for the stadium-jumping class. But she pushed everything out of her head and let the Owl do his magic at the jumps. And he was magical—his stride was perfect and he took every jump as if he had wings. With perfect rhythm he strode into the next and the next and the next smooth jump. Kate knew, even before the judges had posted them, that she and the Owl had gotten high scores.

Dara and Arpeggio followed. They were fantastic—too fantastic. The big, regal gray sailed over the jumps like the wind. Kate wasn't at all surprised—or displeased—when Dara's scores tied with hers for first.

Cross-country was the next, and for Kate and Night Owl the easiest part. Night Owl took the course like he was born to run it. He raced along the narrow, twisting trails and took the jumps effortlessly. It was as if he had set out to prove just how good he really was.

When Kate finally took Night Owl to the van for his last brushing-down before loading, she was feeling a hundred percent.

Her father and Pete were waiting at the van with Jessie. Bruce and Monica had left just before the cross-country test.

Her father hugged her hard. "From what I saw of your cross-country, I'd say you and the Owl are a shoe-in for high score, Katie May."

"Absolutely!" Jessie agreed.

Pete just looked at her as if she was the most wonderful thing he'd ever seen.

"Any news on the dressage scores yet?" Kate asked as she dismounted and led Night Owl up to the rear of the van.

Jessie immediately started untacking him. "Nothing yet."

Pete was doing his best to help Jessie, taking the saddle when she handed it to him and loading it in the van. "What about the scores for the cross-country?" he asked.

"That," Jessie said, "always takes time. There are different judges at different parts of the track, and they all have to get together afterward and—"

"Katie May," Marc Wiley said, "we've got to get a move on here if we're going to get back to the stable in time to go to the hospital this evening." He nodded across the parking field. "Arpeggio's coming in now."

Kate turned to see Dara leading Arpeggio. Mrs.

Cooper was at her heels, saying, "Just get that horse ready for the van, and we'll discuss this at home." She gave everyone a curt nod, and huffed off to find her car.

Dara led Arpeggio up to Night Owl and began untacking him. *"C'est la mère,"* she said. "She's still in a snit about the dressage scores not being posted yet. And she's not too happy that we tied in stadium jumping either. Thinks I should've had the only high score."

"And what do *you* think?" Kate said, watching her carefully. "About you and me tying in the jumps?"

Dara cocked her head and gave Kate one of her lazy grins. "It's only one event," she said.

By the time they had the horses loaded in the van, the dressage scores still hadn't been posted. Kate knew that it would be another fifteen minutes or so before the cross-country scores were in, too.

Dara and her mother had gone to the judges' offices to see if they could learn anything, and hadn't yet returned. Kate looked anxiously at her watch.

"Come on, Kate," Marc Wiley called as he hoisted himself up into the driver's seat of the oversized van.

"Look," Pete said, laying a hand on Kate's arm, "why don't I hang around here and get the scores? I can call you and tell you. What's the number at the hospital?"

"You'd do that?" Kate asked. She almost hugged him!

Jessie tugged at her other arm. "He'll do it," she said. "Now, come on, I'll go back to the farm with you and take care of the horses."

Kate hurriedly gave Pete the number of the hospital. Then, before she could move away, he let his hand slip up her arm, to her shoulder. "Did I tell you how great you looked today?" he said. And he kissed her. Right there in the parking lot, where everyone could see, he leaned forward and kissed her, then backed away.

It was probably one of the shortest kisses in the history of kissing. But it was Kate Wiley's first kiss.

Anne Wiley was sitting up in bed when Kate and Marc Wiley got to the hospital. Kate was still in her jodhpurs and jacket.

"So? How did it go?" Anne asked.

"A tie with Dara Cooper for high score in stadium jumping," Kate reported. "That's as much as we know."

"But Kate was terrific today," her father said.

Perched on the edge of her mother's bed, Kate said, "And so was Night Owl."

The telephone at the bedside jangled. Anne reached for it, but Kate grabbed the receiver before her mother could pick it up.

"Kate!" It was Pete's voice. Kate blushed, thinking again of their kiss. "I've got them—the scores. I mean, it was a real wait. You know something? They still didn't have the dressage scores when they posted the cross-country ones, and—"

"Well?" Kate asked, trying not to sound as impatient as she felt. "So what are my scores?"

"Just a minute—okay. Now, get this," and he read off the score for cross-country.

Kate whooped with joy—she'd gotten the only high score in cross-country.

"And dressage?" she asked, feeling her heart begin to pound.

"Well, you did pretty well," Pete told her, "but—"

"But Dara's was the high score," Kate finished.

"If you really want to know—Dara got two points more in the dressage. But—"

"Two whole points?" Kate moaned. "Jeez! She wasn't *that* good."

"But," Pete went on, "you got two whole points higher than she did in cross-country. So it's an all-around tie."

Kate took this in silently. A tie. She and Dara had tied for first.

"Look," Pete said, "I know the points really matter to you, but for whatever it's worth, Kate Wiley, *I* think you're the best."

"Thanks," Kate answered softly. She suddenly wished her parents weren't listening, but she knew that there was something she had to tell Pete anyway. "You know," she confessed, "even though I was ready to kill Jessie when she invited all of you to the show, I'm really glad you were there today."

"You like having throngs of devoted fans?" he teased.

"No, really. You helped me. You helped a lot."

"Then do something for me and say you'll go to the movies with me next weekend."

Kate heard her father clearing his throat in the background and realized that her parents were still waiting to hear the judges' scores. It really wasn't fair to keep them in suspense.

"I'd like that," she told Pete softly. "And I'll see you in school." She smiled as she hung up the phone.

"Well," her father observed dryly, "the scores can't be that terrible if you're looking so starry-eyed."

Kate giggled as she gave him the news. "It was a tie," she announced. "Dara and I tied for first."

"Sweetie!" her mother cried, holding out her arms to her. "I knew you could do it!"

"And on her own, too," her father added proudly.

"Not exactly," Kate said, thinking of all the support she'd gotten from Jessie and Pete and Dara. Even Monica had helped break some of the tension. She gave her mom a hug. "But it sure is going to feel great when I get my coach back."

Mrs. Wiley reached for her husband's hand. "So what did Mr. Yon's students have to say?" she asked gently.

"Mostly, 'When is Mrs. Wiley going to be back on her feet so we can take lessons?'" Marc Wiley grinned. "And we have the kid here to thank for all the new business."

Kate opened the barn door and slipped inside. It was velvety dark except for the bands of moonlight coming in through the high windows. She walked past Time-Out's stall and checked to see that the mare was sleeping quietly. Nearby, Arpeggio moved restlessly. "Hi, champ," she whispered to him. "You did good today."

At Night Owl's stall she rested her arms on the door and stood gazing at him. He came over to her and blew softly on her arms. She stared at him for a long time, and the only thing she could think to say was, "I love you."

Back out on the path, she stopped for a moment to look up at the sky. The night was clear and filled with stars. Kate felt a rush of sheer happiness. This morning she'd thought her whole world was falling apart. And tonight everything was better than it had ever been before. I think it's going to be a good season, after all, she told herself.

GLOSSARY

BIT. A metal bar that is fit into the horse's mouth to help control the horse's direction and speed.

BRIDLE. Headgear consisting of head and throat straps, bit, and reins. Used for controlling a horse.

CANTER. A rolling three-beat gait, faster than a trot.

CINCH. A sturdy strap and buckle for securing the saddle.

CRIB. A type of bin used to hold food for stable animals.

CROSS-COUNTRY. A race that takes place on open land. These courses include riding across fields, through woods, and along trails, and require jumping over natural and man-made barriers such as ditches, logs, and hedges.

CROSS-TIES. A pair of leads, one attached to the right side of the halter and one to the left, used for holding the horse in place while grooming.

Curry. To brush and clean a horse with a *currycomb,* which is a metal comb.

Diagonal. In dressage, refers to the rider's position when posting to a trot on a circle. The rider would be rising in the saddle as the horse's outside shoulder moves forward and inside shoulder moves back. This keeps the rider from interfering with the horse's balance and freedom of movement.

Dressage. A traditional system of complex maneuvers performed in an arena in front of one or more judges. The test is scored on each movement and on the overall impression that horse and rider make.

Eventing. Also known as *combined training* and *three-day eventing.* A series of tests combining dressage, jumping, and cross-country competitions.

Fetlock. A projection bearing a tuft of hair on the back of a horse's leg, above the hoof.

Filly. A female horse less than four years of age.

Foal. A horse under one year of age. Also, to give birth to a horse.

Gaits. General term for all the foot movements of a horse: walk, trot, pace, canter, or gallop.

Gallop. An extended canter; the horse runs at full speed.

Groom. To clean and care for an animal. Also the person who performs these tasks.

Halter. A loose-fitting headgear with a noseband, and

head and throat straps to which a lead line may be attached.

HANDS. A unit used to measure a horse's height; each hand equals 4 inches. A horse is measured from the ground to his withers. Ponies are 8 to 12 hands high; larger horses are around 16. A 15-hand horse stands 5 feet high at his withers.

HOOF PICK. A piece of grooming equipment used to gently clean dirt and stones from between hoof and horseshoe.

IN AND OUT. Two fences positioned close to each other and related in distance so that the horse must jump "in" over the first fence and "out" over the second.

JODHPUR. Riding breeches cut full through the hips and fitted closely from knee to ankle.

JUMPING. In eventing, also known as *stadium jumping*. Horse and rider must jump and clear ten to twelve fences in a ring. Points are given for grace and height of jump.

LEAD. The piece of rope used to lead a horse.

MUCKING. To clear manure from a horse stall.

OXER. A jump or obstacle that requires the horse to jump its width as well as its height.

PADDOCK. An enclosed outdoor area where horses are saddled and exercised.

PACE. A two-beat gait in which the legs on the same side of the horse move in unison.

POST. Rising up and down several inches out of the saddle in rhythm with the horse's trot.

SADDLE FLAPS. Decorative side pieces on a dressage saddle. They hide the straps needed to keep the saddle in place.

SERPENTINE. In dressage, a series of equal curves from one side of the ring's center line to the other. The horse changes the direction of his turn each time he passes over the center line.

STIRRUP-LEATHERS. The strap used to suspend a stirrup from a saddle.

TACK. The gear used to outfit a horse for riding, such as saddle, halter, and bridle.

TROT. A two-beat gait faster than a walk, in which the horse's legs move in diagonal pairs (left move forward, right remain in rear).

WITHERS. The ridge between a horse's shoulder bones. The highest point above the shoulders where the neck joins the back.

Here's a look at what's ahead in A HORSE OF HER OWN, the second book in Fawcett's "Blue Ribbon" series for GIRLS ONLY.

Northern Spy's conformation was perfect. At least Jessie could find no fault with it. He had a fine head, with large bright eyes and an alert expression. His back was strong and just long enough to be right, the ribs wide behind the girth. His hindquarters were rounded, blending into strong muscular thighs, and all of it was contained in a coat of chestnut satin.

Besides the obvious physical perfection, there was some magic about Spy you couldn't put your finger on. All you could tell when you looked at him was that he was an extraordinary horse. When he was duded up in his braids and polished tack, he would be hard to equal.

And riding this fantastic example of horse flesh would be—*ta-da*—Jessica Claire Robeson.

Lease Spy. The words had been circling in Jessie's brain all afternoon, ever since Kate had first spoken them. Lease Spy and he can be your horse. Jessie took a deep breath and looked out the school bus window, watching the stores of downtown Smithfield give way to houses.

Leasing Spy would mean she'd have to ride him ... a lot. Maybe that was good. Maybe she'd get to understand his moods better, and he'd be easier for her to control.

But that would be hard work. She'd have to spend the rest of her life at the barn for that to happen, Jessie thought morosely. And she'd never get to do anything else—including seeing her family. It was bad enough sacrificing so much of her social life to horses, but to sacrifice her family life, too. . . . Her little sister, Sarah, sometimes talked wistfully about how she hardly ever saw Jessie. How would Sarah feel if Jessie had to spend even more time away from home?

"We'll set the eventing circuit on its ear!" Kate had said. Jessie imagined Kate, Dara, and herself piling up one blue ribbon after another. She'd hang hers in Sarah's room, and the little girl would be thrilled.

Then what was the matter with her? Why didn't Kate's idea of leasing Mr. Yon's horse fill her with joy? Why wasn't she jumping at the thought of calling Mr. Yon to see what could be arranged?

Because you're dumb! Jessie scolded herself, sitting up straighter in the bus seat. This is what you've always said you wanted—a horse to ride and event. Now would you please stop being such a wet blanket about things?

When she got home, Jessie told herself sternly, she was going to race over to the barn to exercise Spy—and show him who was boss. Then she was going to tell her father about the whole idea. *Then* she'd call Mr. Yon and see what he said. Got that? she asked herself.

At least Kate would be happy. Jessie smiled slightly, imagining how pleased Kate would be tomorrow when Jessie casually told her, "By the way, I spoke to Mr. Yon last night, and he's working out the details of a lease." Kate would scream and hug her, and they'd dance around like two crazy people.

It would certainly be perfect if all this worked out, Jessie thought.